The King's Champion
Book One

Xina Marie Uhl

ISBN-13: 978-1-930805-26-2

The first book in a fantasy series of swords, sorcery, and adventure.

A generation ago, a great war convulsed Cantwin. Amidst blood-soaked battles the Stormlifter kings rose up to save the kingdom by imprisoning the dark god Moleck in hell for all eternity.

Or so they thought.

Seventeen-year-old Lance thinks his life is just about perfect now that the prettiest girl in the village wants him. Sure, he dreams of fighting far off battles, but that's nothing more than a fantasy. Until the elders order him away to find a name for himself.

In the dazzling capital, Lance navigates court intrigues with Prince Kieran's unlikely friendship. Yet the glitter and gold obscures a dark conspiracy. Soon the two friends find themselves propelled to the edges of the world on a desperate quest. The stakes: Lance's life, Kieran's throne, and the survival of the Land itself.

Hunted by assassins, and haunted by the awakening of a strange and frightful power within them, they must find proof of Kieran's claim to the throne before a dark god's vengeance destroys them all. For the Power is summoning a champion, and it will not be denied.

DEDICATION

To Dave, who always believes in me

Chapter One

Take it from me. Adventuring all by yourself *sounds* better than it really is.

First, there's the hunger. Just how many rutabagas and strips of dried pork can you carry? Not more than a week's worth. Hunting and gathering may yield a scraggly bunny or two and a few handfuls of raisins shriveled and dried on the vine, but that's nowhere near enough.

Then, there's the confusion. I lost the trail several times despite the map Father had scratched out on a deer hide back in my village.

I hardly need to mention the general discomfort of sore feet, attacking chiggers, rancid waterholes, and the disturbingly close howls of wild beasts as I tried to sleep.

Last night, thunderstorms were added to the list. Specifically, crashing, freezing, hide-in-a-cave and shiver-all-night thunderstorms that leave mud puddles everywhere.

I tripped and skidded into one of these puddles right after spotting the three riders. They were heading toward me. I leapt to my feet, not even taking time to curse over the soaking.

When he drew close enough, a large, dark-faced fellow a few pounds too heavy for the comfort of his horse boomed, "Ho there, young sir!" He smiled. "Taking a bath, are you?"

"Err ... ho there!" I called, grinning like an idiot and waving so energetically that water sprayed in ten-foot arcs from my sodden shirt.

How I longed for companions on my lonely journey! Or, failing that, at least a shared meal. The only other person I'd met on the road so far was an aging prostitute riding a sway-backed mule. She tried to trade her body for some of my rutabagas. I couldn't have run away any faster if my hair were on fire.

The riders each wore scraggly, faded leathers. Their unshaven faces and dirty, weary-looking mounts told me that they had been traveling for a while. Not that I looked much more respectable, with mud dripping off my tangled hair and sluicing down my shirt and breeches.

Where were my manners? I gave the traditional greeting. "Well met in Shaddai's peace."

They formed a semi-circle around me. The one who had hailed me lost his smile. "Shaddai's peace? A pox on it!"

Alarm squeezed low in my gut. The man on the speaker's right had orange-red hair and an explosion of freckles dotting his face and arms. The third man was swarthy, likely a desert dweller, the first I had seen.

"Look, it's one of them cowardly farmers from the Golden Hills," Red-hair sneered. "Out picking flowers for your mommy, whelp?"

My eyes narrowed. In so few words, he had managed to insult my people, my land, and my mother.

I swallowed my temper and gave the wanderers one more chance to prove themselves. "What do you want?"

"Why, bastards like you." Red-hair smiled.

My face flamed. Without thinking, I uttered a hoarse cry and flung myself upon the rider, knocking him from his horse. I beat away at his mid-section, landing several powerful blows before the others hauled me off him and held me, struggling, by each arm.

The beefy one pulled my sword from the scabbard and examined it, holding the blade like a veteran.

"Old, but the blade is good. It's not a bad piece. See if he has anything else, Makai."

The swarthy man plucked my hunting knife from my belt. He ran his finger across the blade. I smiled when a thin line of blood appeared.

"Sharp," he commented stoically. Then he dug through my pack, tossing aside my extra tunic, cook pots, and other gear with disdain. "No coins." He regarded me without expression. "What should we do with him?"

"The altars in the east might want him," Red-hair commented.

The beefy one roughly grabbed my chin and looked into my eyes. "It's worth a try. He looks young enough to make a good sacrifice."

My heart constricted. Around the hearth on cold nights, the Elders had told horror stories, mostly children's tales, I had thought, about a dark religion that bathed itself in human blood. The followers of this evil had instigated the Great War twenty years prior, but since their defeat, they had disappeared. Or, so we had all believed. Shaddai help me, but I didn't want to see one now. I roared and thrashed around, propelled by a surge of panic.

"Get out the kantas root!" someone yelled.

They shoved a bitter, dry plant into my mouth. I choked and gagged, whipping my head around until they held me securely and forced the awful thing down my throat. Limbs suddenly frozen, I kicked spasmodically and ground my teeth together. My body jerked and trembled, and my spasming neck propelled my head straight into the beefy one's bulbous nose. He swore at the contact and slapped my face. A trickle of dark red blood ran from his nostril.

They tied my hands and threw me to the ground. I lay perfectly still, the cool mud pressing against my cheek, while the others set about preparing their supper, which was some sort of disgusting smelling soup. At home, we had used the kantas root as a poison to keep small animals from our fields, but eaten in sufficient doses, it produces a paralyzing effect for up to several days. Smaller quantities, however, result in mild drunkenness. My friends and I had discovered this while chewing it in secret behind the smokehouse. Despite what I'd led my assailants to believe, the drug had hardly affected me, save for a slight throbbing headache. The brigands must have done this to other unfortunates because they paid little attention to me, thinking I was incapacitated.

My adopted father had warned me about my temper more than once. "You're not a bastard to us, Lance," he would tell me. "You're as much our child as the others."

He and my adopted mother had always treated me as such, too. They didn't care that someone had dumped me, squalling and alone, in the wheat fields north of Lor when I was no more than six months old. The only clue to my identity was a broken lance plunged into the ground next to my naked body. A single red flag had been tied to it. They had taken me in, and they called me Lance in recognition of my mysterious origin.

Perhaps one day, I would find the answers about my birth. If I managed to live through the night and whatever plans these devils had in store for me.

The three must have come from town. They guzzled down a jug of something and bragged about who was the better fighter.

Red-hair lurched to his feet and slurred, "Just try to best my blade, fools! I'll prove my sperity—superity—how good I am!" He waved my sword in a wild arc.

The other two didn't bother to get up from their spots next to the fire.

"Shut up and go to sleep, you idiot," Beefy advised.

Red-hair blinked slowly. "You bastards . . . I'll show you." He proceeded to bring the blade down with such force that it struck the log next to my head and wedged there. Now my father's blade had even more dents and dings in it.

"Damn you!" I yelled, which really came out something like, 'Dum ew,' due to the slow paralysis of my mouth and the excess drool that had resulted from it.

Grunting and heaving, Red-hair tugged and yanked at the sword until it came out of the log with a screech. The effort made him fall to his knees next to me, breathing hard. He narrowed his eyes.

"What did you say to me, you stupid prig?"

He grabbed my tunic around the neck and hauled me close to his wide, sweaty face, shaking me for emphasis. I took the opportunity to get rid of my drool by spraying it all over that face. The resulting blow to the side of the head and kicks in the stomach were worth it.

Red-hair lost interest in me after a while and staggered back over to the fire. He blathered on for a while about his heroic ancestors before sagging into a stupor. The beefy one curled up on the ground and went to sleep soon thereafter, but Makai stayed up, standing watch.

By now, muzziness clouded my head. If I waited much longer, I would truly become incapacitated. I steeled myself by repeating the word, *courage*, in my mind before rising to my feet as quietly as possible. With his back to me, Makai toyed with a stick and

hummed a tune. His occasional sways told me the
alcohol had affected him as well.

At first, the solid earth beneath my feet felt
unstable. I walked a few steps forward without
making a sound. When I stood right behind him,
Makai straightened and whipped around just in time
to meet my kick to the head. I gave it all I had, and it
connected perfectly. He fell to the ground with hardly
a sound. Unbalanced by my bound hands, I fell as
well.

Head spinning, I lurched to my feet again. My
pack lay in pieces everywhere. The beefy man had
pocketed my knife, and my sword lay in Red-hair's
slumbering grip. Shaddai! I *couldn't* leave my father's
sword.

I crept forward and, crouching awkwardly,
grabbed the hilt with my bound fingers. Standing
took a while. Beefy gave a loud snore but didn't wake.
Stumbling a few steps away, I tried to think what to
do. With my hands tied behind my back, I couldn't
mount a horse, so I did the next best thing.

I ran.

Well, all right. I lumbered and staggered in
something approximating a run. When I made it out
of sight of my captors, I rubbed the rope around my
wrists against the blade of the sword. After what
seemed like an eternity of sweating and trying, I
managed to free my hands.

I looked back at the dim glow of the campfire I'd
just left. Curses! How I hated to leave without my
gear, but taking a chance at retrieving it was
foolishness. Besides the sword, I carried the thing I
treasured the most—the red flag found at my birth. I
kept it in a pocket over my heart.

I ran until I thought my heart would burst and my head would pop. Now that the blood was coursing through my veins, I felt the effects of the root manifesting. Vomiting it up hardly seemed worth the trouble since it had already been several hours since I'd taken it.

With dogged determination, I walked on, following the bright moon and forcing myself to concentrate on keeping my legs moving. I tried to stay on harder surfaces, like long stretches of rock or gravelly streambeds, to avoid leaving tracks in the drying mud from the recent rainstorm.

I yawned. Once, twice. *Keep going*, I told my legs. *Keep going!* I counted my footsteps, but I kept losing track of the numbers. I had never been much good with figures anyhow.

Dreams and memories chased me. I tried to focus on the ground and the dimly lit shrubs and rocks in my way, but my mind kept straying home, to Shannon.

Shannon, bright-eyed and golden-haired. The most beautiful girl in Lor and, I was quite certain, the rest of the world. I had been in love with her for as long as I care to remember.

Every young male in Lor practically tripped over himself for her notice, but she ignored them all with a lift of her chin. When I happened to catch her looking at me one day as I hefted sacks of grain from my father's cart, I assumed that I'd put my tunic on backward or my hair was sticking up at an odd angle. But then she smiled at me as I hauled my youngest brother, Shay, back home from the creek by the ear. After all, Mother had been calling him for half an hour. I returned Shannon's smile, a little dazed. Shay, the imp, took advantage of my distraction to kick me in the shin. I got revenge by tossing him over my shoulder and ignoring his outraged squirming.

That evening at dinner, I could scarcely stop grinning. Shannon had noticed me at last! Life, so routine and normal, had changed all at once, like an earthquake opening a chasm beneath my feet. Surely, this meant great things to come!

The next morning, the elders called me into the council and relayed their decree. I must leave Lor. In time, if Shaddai willed it, I could return.

The council had always dealt fairly with me before, so I did not argue with their decision. I made ready to go.

On the night before my journey began, I crept out of the house and wandered the moon-touched village, passing homes I knew like my own. Pausing at the well in front of Shannon's dark, sleeping house, I drew a cool cup of water. She lay inside, asleep in her bed, her long blonde hair spread out across the pillow. When I returned, she would probably be married to one of my lucky peers. The thought twisted my insides.

I don't know how long I watched, but suddenly, a shadow detached itself from the house and came toward me. It had a female form. Shannon!

"Hello, Lance," she said, shy and sweet.

A lump obstructed my throat.

"I couldn't sleep. I saw you watching me."

We stared at each other in an awkward silence.

I wanted to spill out a hundred things, about how I thought of her always and how beautiful she was, but instead, I fumbled the cup of water and spilled it on my foot.

She didn't seem to notice. Instead, she bit her lip and looked aside. In a small voice, she said, "You are leaving, and we might never see each other again."

An irresistible emotion expanded in my chest.

"Shannon," I breathed, and before I could reason myself out of it, I moved forward and kissed her.

She responded with a warmth and passion that surprised me. Wrapping my arms around her slender back, I felt her breasts against my chest and her breath on my face. An aching sort of desperation came over me. Tonight was all we had together, all we might ever have.

We pulled apart and stood looking at one another, breathing in ragged bursts. Then, as if in a dream, Shannon curled her fingers around mine and we moved as one to the apple grove. With feverish passion, I sought to smell her skin, touch it, and feel it on mine. It was, I discovered, the same for her.

Now, as I plodded through the dark night, it occurred to me that I should probably stop and determine where I was going. I had no idea of the direction in which I fled. Yet, my legs kept moving and I allowed the momentum to carry me on.

Later, when the sun had risen, I stopped and looked at the sky and the endless lengths of Land rolling in front of me. I wasn't in any shape for reckoning from the position of the sun or the sight of the mountain range—in fact, I could barely focus my eyes to see what was in front of me—so I walked on instead. My arms and legs felt numb, but somehow, that didn't concern me.

I don't know how much time went by—at most, possibly another day, for I vaguely remember night falling again. I remembered nothing else save one muddled instance. Someone bent over me, and a hand grasped my chin and raised my head. A blurry face stared into mine. Alarm clawed at my mind, but I couldn't seem to summon the energy to struggle.

After a moment, I could no longer keep my eyes open. The world drifted away and I knew no more.

Chapter Two

Pain. Fever. Nausea and confusion.

I tried to pull myself back to wakefulness several times, but I could only thrash weakly before succumbing to sleep again. Once, I dreamed that someone sat nearby, bent over a lyre, with silver moonlight limning his dark form. Music glided from the strings, sad and pure and sweet. It stilled me, a healing balm for my tired, sick body. The vision fled under the darkness of deep sleep.

An unknown length of time later, I blinked in the brightness of daylight, my eyes watering until they adjusted. I lay in a thick grove of oak and chestnut trees, cushioned on dry, crinkled leaves. The place looked nothing like the hill country I'd traveled through. How far had I walked? My stomach felt like it had been wrung out to dry. My head and throat didn't feel much better. I groaned, mostly to make sure I still could, and a wretched little peep came from my throat.

"Ah, you are awake at last," a male voice said.

Alarmed, I bolted upright and grabbed around for my sword. I found it lying right next to me. Snatching it up, I threatened the figure who spoke to me. A dizzy rush of weakness overcame me. I watched helplessly as my sword arm sagged to the ground. In a moment, so did the rest of me.

When I regained my wits again, I lifted my head to see a youth about the same age as myself across a smoldering fire. He crouched with his elbows balanced on his knees and smiled at me with the sort of gentle indulgence one bestows on fools or children. Slender and well-dressed in dark blue breeches and a gray tunic, he had dark, almost black hair and bright blue eyes that shone like jewels in the scepter of a king. They were the most striking, intense eyes I had ever seen.

"What?" I got out.

I noticed, now, that a blanket had been tucked around me. The nauseating smell of soup wafted over from a pot on the fire. The young man's pack lay next to him, a finely tooled leather affair. He appeared to be alone and on foot.

"There was music last night," I said, thinking out loud. "You?"

He gave a little nod. "I didn't know you heard. You've been asleep since I found you yesterday afternoon."

I gave another try at sitting up, and I made it this time.

"You stayed," I said, still dazed.

He gave an amused little shrug. "It seemed the polite thing to do." He had a fine, cultured voice with the hint of a northern accent. I took him for the son of a wealthy merchant or perhaps some minor noble.

It suddenly occurred to me how rude I sounded. "Forgive me. Three outlaws attacked me the other day. I barely escaped with my life. I suppose the experience has left me rather suspicious."

"It's quite understandable. Traveling alone can be dangerous. You are headed to Citadel?"

Upon leaving Lor, I had naturally gravitated northwest toward Citadel, the largest city in Cantwin, where King Rodell sat enthroned. There, flanked by a harbor on one side and the lush hills of the Wine Valley on the other, lay the trading center of the country and, most interesting to me, the huge stone castle—the Citadel—that had given the city its name. Stories told that it towered as high as the clouds and stretched the length of a dozen farming fields, a massive stone wonder that persevered, unbreached, for hundreds of years. Such edifices had been built long ago with stones quarried from the deep. Nowadays, no one dared to damage the Land in such ways.

Around Citadel, the nobles, with their handsome estates, lay clustered like grapes on the stem, farming the rich soil. We in Lor, like most of the small villages in the south, paid tribute to the traveling tax collectors once a year. Otherwise, we had little to do with the ruling class. We remained, bordered by wheat fields and prairie, blue sky and brown earth, with Shaddai as our master and the Land as our sustainer.

"Yes, headed to Citadel," I said, then reconsidered. "At least I was."

"Don't worry. You're nearer than you think. I'm going there as well. We can make the trip together if you'd like."

"Yes!" I said, enthusiastic and relieved to have friendly company.

He smiled, leaned forward, and stirred the pot. "Hungry?"

The mere thought twisted my stomach. I shook my head.

"Thirsty, then?" He held out a water skin.

This I accepted. The water tasted good, and I drank half the skin.

When I handed it back, I said, "Thank you. And thank you for aiding me. I am Lance of Lor."

It is customary to give both one's last name and the village of one's birth. Unless one happens to be a bastard, such as myself, with no last name to give. For that reason, meeting someone new has always brought dread and nausea.

"Well met. I am Kieran."

I waited, but he gave no last name or village. An uncomfortable silence sprang up. I cleared my throat and, feeling the need to say something, commented, "You are named after the prince, then?"

He looked at the ground, then said with mild cheerfulness, "Yes. You could say that."

A wave of great weariness dragged at me. I studied Kieran. Something to do with his aspect, or nature, told me to trust him. Completely. What did it matter that he kept silent about his identity? He must have had his reasons.

I lay back down. The hard ground felt good to my aching head and tired muscles.

"A little more sleep, I think, before I'm ready to start out."

"Of course." His voice sounded distant.

Try as I might, I couldn't form the words for a reply.

I slept off and on until the following morning, when I wakened to see Kieran crouching at the fire, turning a spit which contained a delicious-smelling rabbit. My appetite had returned with a vengeance.

Kieran stuck his knife in the roast and, apparently satisfied that it was done, removed it from the spit and placed it in the empty cooking pot to cool. He handed the pot to me.

"Please, eat. You must regain your strength." He must have noted my reluctance because he thrust the food at me with the assurance, "I've eaten already."

My shriveled stomach did the answering for me. I snatched at the meat, burning my fingers and tongue, and devoured it like a starving mongrel. I picked the bones clean and sucked them for the last trace of flavor. The freshly roasted meat, though gristly and rather tough, tasted better than fine cakes and sticky sweets.

When I finished, Kieran gestured to a burlap sack, on top of which lay a collection of roots he must have gathered before I awoke. "Go ahead."

Unsatisfied hunger urged me to accept his generosity.

Kieran sat across from me, cross-legged, leaning forward and peering at me. "I am lately of Nodenrock, in the north. You say you are from Lor, in the south, where the golden wheat grows. Tell me what it is like, and why you have left it to come here, to this distant place."

His earnest curiosity awakened a sharp pang of homesickness in me. So I did as he requested and told him about Lor, with its rolling hills and wide blue sky, its clear air and rich soil. I told him about the summer thunderstorms that left the smell of wet grass thick in the air and about the busy fall harvests and the dark winter evenings when the elders recited the histories and heritage lines. He listened with such openness that before long, it seemed like we were old friends talking after a long absence, interrupting each other, laughing, and excited to see one another.

At seventeen years, I had reached an age when a man wishes to marry and take an interest in his chosen trade. I could do neither when the Law gives nameless orphans no rights and no recognition. The elders had decreed, then, that I must set out in search of a name for myself. I must leave Lor and wander the earth in search of my destiny, or talent, or some such royal deed that would make me noteworthy. When I had done this thing, I could return to the village council and have my name recorded in the heritage books. Only then would I be a proper adult in the eyes of the Law.

I admitted to Kieran that I traveled to Citadel to find a name. I did not tell him that I was an orphan, a bastard in the eyes of the Law. He could not help but know. All the native inhabitants of Lor were blond, with blue eyes. I had brown eyes and auburn hair. Still, he made no comment on the subject, and for that I was grateful.

Every now and again, he reached into this pack and produced another nugget of food for me—apples, nuts, and barley cakes.

When I had finished at last, he laughed. "You've an appetite!"

I looked with sudden suspicion on his diminished pack. "I didn't ... did I eat *everything*?"

"Not quite." He produced a handful of dried beans. "We have these left." He seemed unconcerned.

"You have seldom lived off the Land, have you, Kieran?" I asked with reproof.

He frowned. "Is it so obvious?" He didn't wait for my reply. "I've been away at university for eight years now."

Eight years. A lifetime!

"What was it like?" I'd never known anyone who had been schooled.

He told me about the northern schools, about the snow and the monks who chanted in the morning before the sun rose and spent the day drilling him with numbers and stories and ideas from dusty old scrolls. He learned how to persuade others via speeches, how to write pleasingly, and the customs of different lands. One of these lands, many days' sailing distance across the Sea of Ages, sent the monks a water clock that measured time with the help of buckets and empty balls and weights. I laughed.

"Why should anyone need a device to tell them the time of day? Neither do I understand how history or numbers help you." It sounded like a load of nonsense to me.

He looked at me with a mix of puzzlement and irritation. "To understand our people and our past and to appreciate our accomplishments and know what great thinkers believe."

"What is the use of all that? What really matters are the cycles of the Land, the sowing and reaping, the raising of children, and following Shaddai's Law. All else is surely..." I searched for a word and finally settled on, "Chaff."

He looked at me as though I'd made some profound utterance. "I've never thought of it like that. You're refreshing, Lance."

"Yes, I am," I agreed and grinned. "Modest, too. And, quite frequently, hungry."

"Not again!"

But I was, very shortly.

Kieran insisted that we stay put for another day so that I might regain my strength. After a half-hearted argument, I agreed. The following morning, I awoke refreshed and alone. Kieran's pack lay nearby. He must have gone to look for food to break our fast.

I went down to the pond, where I sat on a rock in the sunlight and polished my blade. The rhythm, back and forth, again and again, calmed and centered me in a way that thinking never had.

I heard Kieran—a poor woodsman—come up from a hundred yards away. He tossed me a half-ripened apricot and gnawed on one himself. A few moments later, he nodded at my sword.

"You know how to use that thing?"

I knew the rudiments of fighting—cut, slash, parry. What more was there? I had noticed his blade, a fine, shiny piece with decorative scrollwork on the hilt and a tooled leather scabbard. He wore it even now.

"As good as you, I'd wager."

His eyebrows lifted. "Let's see about that."

I gave a bored shrug and climbed off the boulder I'd used as a chair. Immediately, I slid on wet and rotting leaves, nearly slicing my leg in two before he had a chance to do it for me.

Kieran smirked. "Sure you're up to this? Perhaps you are still delirious."

I scowled.

We moved a short distance away to a flat area. Kieran drew his blade in a practiced, nonchalant manner, spreading his legs and bending his knees in a stance that suggested he'd done this hundreds of times.

I chose a similar stance myself. He jumped at me in a blur of motion. His blade met mine with a thunderous clang that sent reverberations up my arm and into my shoulder.

I jumped back in surprise and let fly with a powerful slash. He countered with an agile twist and block. Crowding close, he forced his sword flat against my chest and, using his other arm as well, shoved me backward with such force that I nearly stumbled. Taking advantage of my momentary imbalance, he battered me with a series of quick, powerful blows that I clumsily countered. The bewildering array of strikes continued, driving me back until indignation and frustration gave me the strength to plant my left foot and deliver a ringing blow to his side. I stepped close, laying my sword across his chest and shoving him backward in an exact duplication of the move he'd tried on me moments earlier. He staggered, biting off a curse.

I swarmed him in an attempt to repeat the maneuver, but Kieran grabbed my arm, holding me at bay. We lurched around like some clumsy four-footed beast until he finally yanked loose and elbowed me in the jaw. I jabbed him in the ribs with the blade and heard the whoosh of air from his lungs. He then delivered a sharp blow to my thigh, which sent me skidding to the side where I stepped into a gopher hole and tumbled onto my back end.

Kieran came at me, but I scrambled back on my heels and palms, somehow managing to drag my sword along, until I hit a patch of mud and my hands slipped out from under me. I fell flat on my back. When I brought my head up, Kieran's blade prodded my throat.

"An easy defeat," he said, grinning.

"Easy?"

My fist spasmed around a handful of mud. I flung it at him. It struck him in the middle of the forehead. He froze in surprise. Then he tossed his sword aside with a roar and jumped at me.

We wrestled around for a while before somehow ending up in the pond, laughing and splashing each other. When we finally dragged ourselves out, we both collapsed in the grass, dripping wet. His fine clothing was soaked.

"You look like a drowned rat," I observed.

"You're no better." He smiled.

We fell quiet, catching our breaths. He wiped his face off with the edge of his shirt and regarded me.

"Who taught you the sword?"

"No one," I said with a guffaw, thinking that he was teasing me.

"Truly?"

"Truly."

"You must have a natural gift, then."

"I do?"

"Yes, surely." He seemed genuine. "You almost had me once or twice, and I've been training since I was ten years old."

I leaned over on my elbow. I'd always been good at physical endeavors—running, fighting with the other boys, and riding the little wild ponies we sometimes caught. Though lately, a rapid growth spurt had given me long legs that I hadn't quite adjusted to yet, and I found myself tripping and flailing more than usual.

"Please," I said, grinning. "Tell me more about my magnificent natural talents."

Kieran broke off a stick and threw it at me. "The One loves a humble man, Lance. Didn't your people teach you that?"

The One. His use of that term instead of 'Shaddai' piqued my interest.

"Not at all. Tell me what your people have taught you," I prodded.

"My people?" He repeated, taken off guard. He sat up and thought, and his teasing grin slipped away.

Earlier, when he had told me about the area near Nodenrock, where the Land was blanketed in ice and the wolves howled across the frozen expanse, he mentioned that he hadn't wanted to leave, but that his father had called him home for a visit. His mother had been dead for almost a decade. He still seemed quietly troubled by her death. I wanted to ask him more about his family—were they wealthy merchants or minor nobles, and did he have brothers and sisters—but I sensed his reluctance to speak of himself.

"My people taught me much. They taught me honor, duty, responsibility, how to behave mannerly, to speak with culture . . . and how to be alone," he said with bittersweet candor.

Something dark lay behind his words, something not to be dredged into the light of day. After a moment, I made a little noise of assent.

"That must be why you are such a miserable wrestler."

The grin came back, and with it, a slap upside my head. I had to answer the offense, of course. That set off another round of good-natured play that ended with me grinding Kieran's face in the mud.

Kieran had wisely soaked the beans overnight and left them cooking in the coals all day. Later that night, we were able to eat the last of them. After the sun set, we lay wrapped in blankets, staring up through the dark treetops to the thousands of stars clogging the night sky.

"Tomorrow, we'll leave for Citadel," Kieran said. Then, after a pause, "I will miss the quest of the open road and this peaceful place. In Citadel, it is never quiet, even at night when everyone is sleeping. So many people with so many worries. They crowd my mind, even from here."

I didn't know what he was talking about. How could people's worries crowd your mind? Still, his words, or his tone of voice, or perhaps something totally different, touched off a strange recognition within me. A spark, glittering and fearsome. A rushing sound expanded inside my skull. I became aware of a peculiar quality of silence thronging around me, alive, mysterious, and strangely active.

I pressed my palms to the earth, and the invisible currents became stronger. I perceived a great connectedness in the Land, in all people and in every place, among all living things. A well of emotion— sweetness, warmth, and something even deeper and greater—filled my heart. I lifted my hand from the earth, consciously forcing down the overwhelming emotions. What was this? Shaddai's living presence? Is this what the elders were always going on about? I didn't want to understand. I was just an ignorant peasant.

We had been silent for a long time. Kieran probably slept by now. Surely, he had not felt this strange sensation as well. But then he turned his head and looked at me, the whites of his eyes glistening in the dark. Though he said nothing, I had the distinct feeling that he knew what I had just experienced, and he understood it.

I looked away, unsettled, and turned my thoughts to Shannon. She was a more pleasant diversion, though no more understandable. Soon, sleep claimed me.

Chapter Three

In the morning, we packed up and left our campsite. Kieran led the way through the grove, which wound around clumps of brush. The terrain was more difficult to traverse here than it had been on my journey so far. The undergrowth was thicker, the hills higher, and trees taller. After scarcely more than an hour's walk, we climbed a hill, fought our way through the bushes that crowded the crest, and stood at the summit on a jutting promontory of rock, panting and gaping at the valley spread out before us. The twisting silver length of a wide river cut a swath through the Land. On its search for the sea, the river passed on the far side of the largest city I'd ever seen.

Tall stone walls circled a castle, the most unbelievable spectacle of all. A great, gray stone masterpiece loomed high as it watched over its people with stoic regard. The clean, sharp lines and unyielding symmetry of the architecture were unlike anything I'd ever seen—or dreamed of seeing—in the little sod houses of Lor. Groves lay outside the walls toward the east, and elsewhere, neatly manicured green fields and clusters of huts dotted the earth. Stands of post-filled fields covered the hillsides like the quills of a porcupine. Vineyards, Kieran informed me. They would be deep green and bursting with fruit in the fall.

My heart swelled. The vision before me seemed like a dream. I looked at Kieran, having no words. He smiled.

"We've been at the edges of the prince's hunting grounds, just outside of Citadel. I told you we were close."

"Citadel?" I choked. Then, upon recovering, I punched him in the arm. "You didn't tell me we were *this* close."

Beyond Citadel, the sea sparkled in the sunlight, stretching to infinity. The strange algae-like tang of the moist air reached my nose even here.

He shrugged, and we jogged down the hill, following a game trail, which made the trek through the undergrowth much easier. Before long, we came upon the first real road I'd seen on my journey. Together with merchants and farm wives, families, and a grizzled old man herding two fat pigs, we followed the road as it crossed fields, villages, and sun-speckled groves before coming at last to the line of people outside the gates seeking entrance to the city.

I could not tear my eyes from the magnificent stone wall before us—so many perfectly set blocks—while two guards in shiny helmets and red and black livery demanded papers or payment from all the entrants. I had neither, but how could they turn me back after I'd come so far?

When our turn came, however, Kieran simply reached in his pack and produced a golden brooch in the shape of a lion rampant. The guard blinked when he saw it and looked from Kieran to myself.

"He is with me." Kieran jerked a thumb at me.

The guard nodded mutely, and we moved into the city without having to state our names and home villages like everyone else. A moment later, after a furious whispered exchange, one of the guards went running past us, pausing only to flash Kieran a half-panicked backward glance. I looked at Kieran for an explanation, but he volunteered none, saying instead, "Please, I know you haven't a place to stay. Do me the honor of hosting you."

I smiled at his earnest politeness. In all truth, I hadn't thought about my lodging place. "Yes, of course. That incredible honor is yours," I teased.

He snorted a laugh and shoved my shoulder.

The city boiled all around us—close buildings, chaotic noises, and the colors! Gray walls and brown shops and yellow straw-roofed houses, flags of green and red and gold flying from the buildings, and the blue sky over all. And the people! More than I'd seen anywhere—young and old, rich and poor, perfumed and foul-smelling. We rounded a corner onto a cobblestoned street where merchants displayed their wares and haggled with prospective buyers. The array of goods astounded me.

Kieran, smiling at my amazement, pointed them out as we walked—pearls from the island of Seawatch, spices imported from the Port of Sand, jaguar hide from Renik in the Kole Mountains, carved daggers from Verzon City. And more. Fish caught in Citadel's own port, fluffy cakes smothered in clover honey, berry tarts, and leg of lamb cooked in spiced wine. My mouth watered.

"Look!" I cried to Kieran, pointing at three cats dancing on their hind legs around a man playing a flute. "What a place!"

"Yes," he said. "It's busier than I remember, but so much is the same. The tailor's, the sweet shop, the cathedral—"

A shout went up from down the street. A half-dozen men, armed and wearing red and black livery, charged through the crowd, their eyes fixed on us. Surprised into action, I yanked out my sword and brandished it, covering Kieran who stood behind me.

The leader of the group—a brawny, black-bearded man with curly black hair and a matching scowl—stopped in front of me.

Nodding at my sword, he growled, "What do you think you're doing with that battered old field plow, boy?"

I opened my mouth to retort, but Kieran put a restraining hand on my arm and stepped in front of me.

"It's all right, Lance. They are here for me. Carter." He inclined his head toward the leader. "You look the same, even after so many years."

"My prince," Carter replied, bowing. The armed men following him did likewise.

"What?" I exclaimed. "Who . . .?"

Kieran gave a self-deprecating little shrug. I gaped at him for a moment before the truth drew a cold shroud around me.

"You?" I choked. "You're Prince Kieran?"

"I'm afraid so."

I looked around, my stomach churning. "But how? I mean, we traveled together, not very far, but—oh, Shaddai! I ground your face in the mud!" I howled, mortified, then tried to sheathe my blade and instead dropped it on the street.

I prostrated myself before him, face burning.

"None of that," Kieran chided, pulling me upright. "It's all right."

"No, it isn't, my prince," Carter proclaimed, arms crossed. "You're a week later than your message stated. Your father is in a fury."

His father. *The king.* I felt sick.

Then somehow, the guards had surrounded us both and we were hurrying through the city as the crowd parted before us. Kieran asked Carter about a series of people, and I heard the word 'council' a few times, but I stopped trying to listen to Carter's replies when we rounded a corner and the Castle loomed up before us like some majestic mountain peak—quiet and forceful, as high as the sky and just as fine, the whole a confusion of towers and flags, patrolling guards and open windows with gaily-colored curtains billowing in the breeze. The yard before it was huge and filled with burgeoning flowers. Shrubs populated the area near the doorway, and grass extended out to meet the cobbled pathway where we walked. To my right lay a massive courtyard with a bubbling fountain in the middle. The pinnacle of an ornate cathedral jutted up into the sky directly across from it. We walked to the left toward a large, long barrack in front of which a dozen or so men sparred with wooden swords.

"Carter, a moment, please," Kieran said and drew me aside. "Lance, I hoped we would have more time before they found me. I will explain as soon as I'm able. In the meantime, you can stay in the barrack. I'll see that you are attended to."

"My prince—" Carter said impatiently.

"Yes, I suppose. If it's what you want," I murmured in a daze.

Carter hurried him off, but Kieran cast a single, distressed look at me over his shoulder.

My head spun, my heart pounded in my chest, and my thoughts whirled like snowflakes in a blizzard. I watched him go, trying and failing miserably to absorb the enormity of what had just happened.

The sounds of sword fighting awakened me early the next morning. Staggering upright, I dressed, splashed water on my face, and went outside the barrack, yawning.

Carter and the others from yesterday stood on the training field, sparring in groups of two. Carter shouted a suggestion here, an encouragement there, in a loud voice. He glanced over and saw me.

"Boy!" he boomed. "Do you want to try out that half-wrecked twig of a sword I saw you with yesterday?"

"Yes, sir!" I cried, my heart leaping in anticipation.

I ran inside, threw on my boots, and grabbed my sword. Outside, Carter broke up the duo fighting nearest him.

"Kenton, go a round with young Lance here," he told a squat, dark-skinned man nearby.

Kenton looked at me and grinned, revealing a broken front tooth filed to a point like a spike.

"Oh," continued Carter, "and don't go easy on him."

I had only a moment to wonder just what that entailed when Kenton rushed at me, howling. I let out a surprised cry as he launched a stroke designed to chop off my head. Survival instincts flaring, I ducked and elbowed him in the gut. Skittering backward, I let fly with a wild chop that sliced clean through a hank of Kenton's thick, dark hair. The men standing around us abruptly fell silent.

Kenton froze, then put a hand to his hair in dull surprise. He turned to me with a snarl of rage.

"I will chop you up into little pieces for that, boy."

A wild exhilaration filled me. "Try, and I'll trim your whole head!"

Kenton gave another roar and unleashed a vicious round of blows at me. I fended them off with limited success, catching a jab in the ribs, a slap on the arm, and a ringing swipe to the head. I managed to get in a good swat to his right side, unbalancing him. Backing up quickly, I found myself near the barrack wall. Shaddai! I took a few steps forward, trying to reposition myself.

Kenton snorted like a mad bull and pawed the earth. Lowering his head, he ran at me, powerful legs pumping his body forward with tremendous speed. I believe he intended to hit me in the stomach and knock the wind out of me. That might have worked if I hadn't twisted aside at the last instant. Kenton hit the barrack wall head on. He sprawled on the ground, semi-conscious.

The others surrounded me, laughing and patting me on the back. Carter came up also, looking a smidgeon less foreboding than usual.

"Good job, lad."

I looked worriedly at Kenton's inert figure. "Is he . . .?"

"Oh, don't fuss about him. Marl, Uffen, haul Kenton over to the physician. He'll be all right. He's strange about his hair, that's all."

"Well, do you believe me now, Carter?" a familiar voice said.

"Kieran!" I blurted out. "I mean, my prince."

Flustered, I gave a clumsy bow.

Kieran approached, grinning. He looked more princely today with his hair combed and face washed, wearing a matching dark blue doublet and breeches. He had, I realized for the first time, the handsome visage—dark hair, blue eyes—for which the Stormlifter dynasty was famous.

Kieran nodded at Carter. "I told him, Lance, about your talent for fighting."

"Aye, my prince," Carter acknowledged, giving me a critical eye. "He's a sturdy young man with a good arm and quick reflexes. I'll train him if you wish."

I gawked at Carter.

Kieran was looking at me. "Excuse us, please, Carter?"

Carter nodded and moved off a few yards, where he stood with a couple of the men, watching us.

"Lance, allow me to explain myself."

I lowered my eyes. "No need, my lord—"

"Please," he said. "Don't treat me as if I am the One himself. Far from it, I am painfully mortal. You must call me Kieran when we're alone."

Surprised, I blurted out, "But—"

"If I wanted someone to fawn over me, I need not travel far. Call me Kieran. That is a great gift to me, to be known for myself and not my position." A quiet rawness in his voice struck me.

"Is that why you didn't reveal your identity sooner?" It made a strange kind of sense.

He looked aside, considering. "Yes, I think so. It has a way of changing everything. I wanted … I'm at a loss to explain myself except to say that there is blessedness in anonymity. In any case, I deceived you. I beg your pardon."

I watched him, not quite knowing what to think. Where was the haughtiness, the disdain of royalty?

"You have it."

"Good." He smiled with relief. "About what Carter said. It is true. I would like you for my guard, if you are willing."

The world spun in lazy, slow circles, and a peculiar weakness drained the blood from my face.

"It is a big decision," Kieran said. "Please, take some time to think about it."

"Of course I'll do it!" I gabbled hoarsely.

He grinned at my enthusiasm and held his hand out for a pledge. I grasped it, numb and amazed.

"Nothing so wonderful has ever happened to me before," I jabbered, then paused, thinking about Shannon . . . well, *almost* nothing so wonderful had ever happened to me before. "I'm just a peasant from a sod hut. Why do you want me on your guard? I'm not *that* good at swordplay."

"You do have a particular talent, Lance. But you're right, that is not the whole reason." He looked up at the cold stone facade of the Castle. "There is another reason that I cannot reveal yet. Right now, I must appease my father. Will you trust me until I can tell you more?"

"Yes, my–Kieran."

"Good." He smiled.

He left then, heading purposefully to the front doors of the Castle. He looked small against the backdrop of all that gray stone.

Carter appeared at my side and observed me, gruff and reluctant, for a long moment. At last, he said, "Who *are* you, boy?"

I shrugged helplessly. "I am no one."

He studied me as if gauging the truth of my words. "Not anymore, young Lance. Now you are the prince's man, and that is no small honor."

I swallowed, well aware of that. Sometimes, though, there are no words. Carter nodded as if he understood, and we walked off together to begin my training.

&

Practicing sword fighting in the Castle yard became a daily occurrence. When we weren't sword fighting, Carter sat me down under an oak tree and pounded me with rules of etiquette and court deportment, which included learning the names and stations of the nobles. I learned to stop gaping at the goings on of the town after Carter had cuffed the back of my head six or seven times.

After the first few days, Carter cranked a strange-looking wooden device into the yard and ordered me to climb all over it, hanging and pulling myself this way and that. He said it would strengthen my muscles, but it seemed like pure foolishness to me. When not busy with me or one of the other men, Carter amused himself by yelling and chastising the armor boys.

"Got to learn them respect somehow," he commented. It was the only time I recall him looking really happy.

One afternoon, Kieran and I went outside the city walls. There, in the full glare of the sun, we sweated and gasped as we sparred with shields and wooden swords. The rest of the guard reclined in the shade of a nearby cedar. Carter had urged us out here to practice in different terrain, a much more enticing prospect a few hours ago, in the coolness of morning.

I lunged for Kieran, trying a backslash move that I couldn't seem to master, when I stepped in a gopher hole—the third time I'd done that today—and crashed to my knees. Instinctively, I grabbed the nearest thing to steady myself—Kieran's leg—and managed to unbalance him, pulling him down as well. A chorus of laughter broke out from beneath the cedar tree. I lay on the ground, too tired and winded to continue the fight with Kieran. After a moment, during which my comrades' laughter became louder, I got up on my elbows and glared in their direction.

"It wasn't *that* funny."

Kieran stood, brushing dirt off his fawn-colored breeches. "Don't take offense, Lance. I doubt they're laughing at you."

"What, then?"

"Better to ask 'who'."

"You?"

"Well, I don't see anyone else out here," he joked, but then he observed my expression. "Don't you know?"

I made a 'tell me more' gesture.

Kieran nodded at the others, too far off to hear our conversation. "They hate me."

I pulled back, surprised. "Where did you get that idea?"

He looked at me as if I was rather dull. "It's nothing new. I'm a poor imitation of Rodell."

"You're mistaken."

He shrugged. Suddenly, unaccountably angry, I jumped up.

"I'll prove it." I stomped over to my fellows and snapped, "Why are you laughing?"

Carter ignored me, Marl and Kenton looked at me blankly, and the others just laughed harder.

I looked back at Kieran. The studied indifference on his face said more than words could.

After that, I began to notice the sly comments, the sneers, and the suspicion—all of it directed at Kieran. I cursed myself as a fool for not noticing sooner.

Once, when I saw Carter scowling after the prince as he walked off the practice yard into the Castle, I confronted him.

"Why do you hate him so, all of you?"

Carter glanced at me in surprise, unaware that I was watching him. He looked annoyed.

"Because he is not one of us."

"What do you mean?"

Carter kicked the dirt, irritated. "I don't know. He's just different somehow, always mouthing off about the One and all, not acting his age. He has lived with those crazy northerners too long to be our native son. He's been gone for years. Then, when he finally does come home, it's with the likes of you."

"I can't speak to why he brought me here, but as for his absence in Nodenrock, he was learning to lead his people."

"He should have been *here*, in his native city, not living in the snow with a bunch of half-crazy monks. King Rodell has ruled for seventeen years. What better example has he than his own father?"

Red rage burned the edges of my eyesight. "Do you resent him because he was schooled elsewhere, or because he would be a fair and gentle king?" I snapped, knowing that Carter might beat me for my impertinence.

"Watch your words, boy. In this kingdom, we want a strong and courageous leader. What do we know of Kieran?"

His excuse held no water. Both Carter and I knew that the prince was, if anything, courageous. I could not imagine him otherwise.

"You know enough not to hate him."

Carter's jaw hardened. "I am the prince's servant, answerable to him above even the king himself. I have given him my vow of honor, and would gladly give him my life, but that doesn't mean I have to like him!" he declared and stomped off.

Chapter Four

Uffen, the most annoying of the guardsmen with whom I shared the barrack, bounded up to my cot early one morning, waking me with the words, "We're at war!"

Fear squeezed my stomach. I sat up straight. "The king has declared it?"

"No, you dolt. A *practice* war. Many of the city guards will join us."

"Not to mention the prince," commented Shar, who stood in front of the open door, scratching his crotch.

I craned my head to see Kieran striding through the yard toward us, followed by Marl and Dirk in their black and red livery. They all wore matching stern expressions. The guards always seemed dour when they watched Kieran. I didn't understand them. Kieran was a fine man—kind and generous, likable and intelligent. He would make a perfect king someday.

Every day, Kieran took time from whatever it was he did in the Castle to join us in the kitchen for dinner or on the practice field for a session at arms. Even though he was the prince, I felt more at ease around him than the others, all of whom, in addition to being several years older than me, seemed, at best, to tolerate me as a stranger.

Half an hour later, thirty of us stood facing each other on an empty field outside the city gates. A crowd of onlookers gathered nearby, gossiping and pointing.

I stood in position, pulling at the collar of my new uniform and glancing nervously at the large muscle-bound hulk facing me. He bared his teeth, revealing a piece of meat wedged there—the remains of his dinner, or the last recruit with scarcely three weeks' training? Shaddai, perhaps, would be gracious and allow me not to shame myself too much.

I happened to look over at Kieran then, separated from me by two men on my right. He offered me an encouraging smile.

Carter gave a shout. We answered with loud, rallying cries and swarmed against each other in an explosion of clashing metal.

I knew after about two sword blows that my opponent was as formidable as he looked. Clumsily, I blocked, parried, and blocked some more just as Carter had taught me, but I could barely ward off his tremendous blows, delivered with devastating precision.

A curious awareness expanded inside my skull. One part of my mind busily defended myself, but another part—the greater part—detached from the situation altogether. Something more important demanded my attention. Above the clamor of sword and shield, I heard sounds I hadn't noticed before. Little wordless exclamations, the shuffle of feet, the onlookers' excited murmurs. My sense of hearing seemed a living thing. It moved and searched, listening for—what? Breath. Labored breath. Yes—I heard it now. I turned, and my eyes went directly to the source.

Kieran, face twisted with effort as he battered furiously against a red-haired devil of an opponent. One of his strikes missed, and the redhead seized the opportunity to jab Kieran in the ribs. He gave an exclamation of pain. The purest feeling of dread for his safety erupted in me. I had never known such a sharp and primal feeling. I *had* to get to him. Hesitating, I blocked yet another powerful blow. In and around the exercises Carter gave me, the practices, and the chores, I remembered his oft-repeated exhortations. *Cowardice is the lowest of all low behaviors. Fear and trembling are acceptable. Running from one's opponent is not. The man who abandons his opponent on the battlefield, though he may live, is dead to honor.* And so on. Carter expected that I should stay put.

But then I saw Kieran's opponent draw back a well-placed strike, and the next moment, I was shoving past the two men between us to get to him. My hulking opponent gave a cry of indignation. I jumped in front of Kieran—somehow managing to avoid his sword—and kicked his opponent in the stomach so hard that he sprawled on the ground. In quick succession, I stomped on his wrist, kicked his sword free, and whirled around, leapfrogging back to my own opponent. With swift brutality, he caught me upside the cheek with the flat of his blade.

I then made intimate acquaintance with the gravel scattered on the field.

I sat on a stool in the barrack, wincing as one of the armor boys dug the gravel out of a scrape on my cheek, when Carter slammed in the door.

Upon seeing me, he paused, wrinkled his brow, and said with characteristic volume, "What in the *hell* was that?"

My athletics had already caused quite a stir among my companions, who at turns congratulated me or marveled at my stupidity.

"I saved the prince, didn't I?"

Carter's face went red. "The *prince* was doing fine on his own."

Kieran sat against the wall and grinned at the exchange between Carter and me. He rose and laid a calming hand on Carter's shoulder. "Don't exert yourself, Captain. Lance is simply showing his enthusiasm. Come, why not let him off for the rest of the day? You haven't given him a rest—even for worship—since he arrived. I'll see that he's kept safe."

Carter frowned, and scowled, and frowned deeper, but at last, he gave a gruff assent.

I jumped up, excited at the prospect of seeing the city. I snagged a cloth from the armor boy and pressed it to my cheek. "That's good enough," I told him and headed out the door, following Kieran.

Kieran stopped short and I, not paying attention, plowed into him. He didn't appear to notice.

A throng of people approached the yard, led by a man who could only be the king. He was perhaps not much taller than Kieran, but he held his head so high and his back so straight he seemed like a giant. His black boots shone in the sun, and a soft, fur-cuffed cape covered part of his doublet and danced mischievously around his calves. Whereas Kieran was slim and lithe, King Rodell was thick and muscled, and he walked with obvious power. A short beard covered his jaw. His black, wavy hair fell to his shoulders and gave him a wild air. I could not discern the color of his eyes. I only knew that they were hard.

The king was heading toward a figure approaching from the south road. The man, slim and dark-haired, wore a dashing scarlet cape with a matching plumed hat.

The king gave a great laugh, flung wide his arms, and called, "Morrigu, you have returned!"

Morrigu removed his plumed hat with a flourish and bowed, an answering smile on his face. A moment later, the two parties met. Kieran fell back beside me, frowning as he beheld the two, talking and laughing animatedly.

"Morrigu?" I asked.

"My father's chief advisor. He just returned from some mysterious mission." He frowned. "I don't recall such an enthusiastic greeting from him at *my* return."

The two gestured and laughed while we looked on. Then the king glanced in our direction and moved toward us. I scarcely knew what to think—I had never been so close to a king!

I bowed as he approached, my heart beating wildly.

"Father," Kieran acknowledged softly.

"Prince." Morrigu's voice was low and a tad mocking.

"Rise, boy," the king said, and it took me a confused moment before I realized that he spoke to me.

I stood and found myself face to face with the king, who eyed me in a critical manner.

In a deep, commanding voice, he said, "Who are you? Your face is not familiar to me."

My stomach clenched. I stared at him for what seemed like a long time before I realized that he expected a reply. Just as I opened my mouth to speak, Kieran interjected, "He is my new guardsman, Lance of Lor."

"You have no surname?" Shaddai, but he had a loud voice!

"Not yet, Your Highness."

"Well, continue to serve my heir with your life as you did on the field today, and you will have earned one."

"Yes, my lord," I replied.

Morrigu smirked, then he turned his head and murmured something to the king about a trade agreement. The king nodded, and the two of them wandered off, absorbed in conversation. I watched the entourage follow them.

When everyone was out of range, Kieran turned to me, his mouth crooked slightly in a grin. "Do you see the family resemblance?"

"No," I said, still recovering from the shock of the encounter. "Same color hair, but that's about it."

"That's what everyone says."

"Why are all those people going along with him?" I asked.

"The curse of royalty. Privacy is a luxury that is often hard to afford, even with all his riches." Then, Kieran shrugged off his tense mood and smacked my leg. "Come on, we can't be dallying."

"Yes, my lord," I said solemnly.

Kieran slid me a dubious sideways glance, and I couldn't help but laugh. He shoved me, and I returned the favor after looking around to see that no one else was watching.

We spent the rest of the day together, roaming the streets. He showed me the nooks and crannies of the city—the shops with the finest pastries and juiciest roasts, the wood carvers' guild, where we sat for an hour, watching as the apprentices nicked their fingers imitating a particularly tricky cut, and the bookseller, who exclaimed in delight upon seeing Kieran. He dragged him to the back to display his latest acquisition—the history of so and so—while I thumbed through volumes disappointingly devoid of pictures.

We ended up in the king's stable, a magnificent place with gold trim, clean stalls, and the finest, longest-legged horses I'd ever seen. Kieran showed me his favorite horse, a soft-eyed mare called Goldie, who whinnied and nuzzled his neck when she saw him. He led her into a pen and let her run in circles, attached to a line. She trotted prettily, her coat glistening in the sun.

As we walked her back to her stall, Kieran asked, "Lance, why did you attack my opponent like that today?"

"It is my duty, is it not?" I hedged.

He looked me in the eyes steadily. "No, not really."

"I ... I don't know. I couldn't *not* do it," I answered honestly. The explanation sounded foolish. I tried to clarify it. "It was as though I knew I must, in the same way I know the seasons change, or I like to eat raspberries, or when you are troubled, you go to the hill overlooking the Wine Valley and sit in the bole of the oak tree—"

Kieran stopped in his tracks and faced me. He blinked once, very slowly, and all the color drained from his face. "How do you know that?"

"About the oak tree? You must have told me."

"No, Lance," he said firmly. "I never told you about my oak tree. I've never told anyone." He turned aside, his breathing shallow.

I was getting more confused by the moment. "But of course you must have! How else would I know?"

"I'm not sure, Lance. But of a sudden, I'm quite certain that when *you* are troubled, you go in your mind to the ocean, smooth and blue and vast. As you saw it once, long ago . . ." He faced me again, his eyes large and bright, his face still.

I couldn't tear my eyes away from him. A headache sprang up in my skull. I knew I had never told Kieran of my love for the ocean. It was too personal, too private. And he *knew* it, just as I had known his personal, private thought.

"This is . . ." I murmured.

"Impossible. Strange. Uncanny," Kieran finished for me.

"Yes, all of those."

An awkward silence sprang up between us. I lifted my hands to my temples to massage away the pain there.

Kieran looked aside, putting his hand over his mouth. Then he turned to me, his face set as if he had made a decision. "Tell me what you know of Moleck."

I blinked. "The dark god? Why?"

"I've heard that those from Lor have much knowledge of Moleck's followers because you fought them so fiercely during the Heathen Wars. Please, tell me what you know."

Although my knowledge seemed useless, full of myth as it was, I told it to him anyway. Many years ago, at the beginning of time, a man lived who despised the holiness of the Land and thirsted for a way to destroy it and glean its power for his own. His name was Moleck and he and his followers ravaged the Land, sacrificing victims and drinking their heart's blood, burning whole villages and filling the soil with deadly poison so that nothing would grow for many years. When Moleck grew old, his earthly body sickened, but he fought against death with all the arcane knowledge he had collected over the years. Many of his followers slit their own throats so that they could bargain with death and take his place. Some say that he did not die, but instead, he cast himself into the wind and still lives today, holding the key to eternity in his wretched hand.

Kieran said nothing for a long moment after I finished speaking.

"I did not come home from school merely because my father summoned me, as I told you."

"Why, then?"

"Something is happening, Lance. Something bigger than both of us, than Citadel, possibly even bigger than the Land itself. The monks in Nodenrock have prophesied. Moleck is returning, they say, brought forth by his followers who are springing from the earth like weeds in springtime."

A chill worked its way around my innards. The elders still spoke of the struggle with the dark god's followers as though it happened yesterday, though it ended almost twenty years ago. The Land had been wiped clean of their cruelty, their bloodthirsty sacrifices . . . or so we thought. The kidnappers who had assaulted me on the way to Citadel . . . they had spoken of the altars in the East. Now I knew what they meant.

"I suspect my father's advisor, Morrigu, is one of them."

I thought of Morrigu, whom I had only seen once earlier today. Something about Morrigu rubbed me the wrong way.

"I have no proof of these suspicions and few allies. You are, I think, one of them."

"That is why you befriended me and put me on your guard," I said, understanding at last. A feeling I couldn't identify drew bands across my chest.

"Not entirely. You do have talent, and I like you. Though I can't deny that I also need someone to watch my back."

"Why go through all the trouble of asking me? I am in your guard—you have simply to order me. I am bound by my duty and my honor, not to mention my station, to obey." It came out more bitter than I intended. Could he even understand? I had thought we were friends, but he was a noble and I was a peasant. Perhaps I had been foolish to trust in what seemed like his earnest desire to bridge that gap.

He looked at me in silence. Then he did an amazing thing. He dropped to his knees in front of me, dark head bowed.

"Upon my honor and my life, I swear that I will never use my place as heir and prince to compel you to obey me. You will always have a choice whether to serve me or not. I will ever honor that choice and you. I so pledge it." He extended his hand to me. "Do you accept?"

I swallowed, stunned. My voice came out as a scratch. "I accept." I grasped his hand and helped him to rise.

He smiled, teeth shining white. "There now. We are bound first and always by ties of friendship."

A great fist seemed to squeeze my throat. Who was I that Shaddai had so blessed me with Kieran's faithful companionship?

"What now?" I got out.

"We will find out the truth," Kieran said with an air of finality that I could not question.

"Be ready. Soon, I will come to you for more help."

Chapter Five

"What, now?" I complained when Kieran shook me awake. "It's the middle of the night!"

"Shh!" He put a hand across my mouth to silence me. I pushed it off.

"Yeah, yeah," I grumbled. I didn't know what he was worried about. Half the men in the barrack slept like the dead, and the other half snored so loudly that I could have driven a team of mules through the middle of the floor without anyone hearing.

"Come on." He took me by the arm and guided my stumbling, bleary-eyed self outside.

Lately, Carter had increased my training with cruel glee. Every day brought something new. First, I ran around the city with a bag of grain flopped across my back. Next, I fought off three men at once. I learned to stitch up my own wounded arm. He forced me to polish my sword and armor four times a day so I would get it 'right.' Then he directed me to throw a weighted rope on top of the city wall and climb it, and so on. I ate four large meals a day and pitched headfirst into my pallet from sheer weariness every night. There was hardly enough time to dwell on the frightening revelations that Kieran had disclosed.

I tromped after Kieran down cobblestone streets that gleamed silver from the light of the near-full moon. Stillness lay like a thick blanket over everything. The only sounds were the occasional yap of a dog and the scuffle of our footsteps. I blinked until the haze had cleared from my eyes. My hand rested on my dagger, ready for what may come.

Kieran turned down one street, then another. I scarcely knew my way around the city in the full light of day. At this hour, I was completely disoriented. At last, he paused by the side of a modest stone storehouse.

I yawned, still dazed from sleep. Kieran helped me wake up by squirting a water skin in my eye. I grabbed the skin out of his hand and returned the favor. After a few moments of scuffling around and jabbing at one another, I found myself coherent. And quite foul-tempered.

"What in Shaddai's holy name are we doing here?"

"We're going in there." Kieran pointed across the way to a large building with a sweeping pinnacle on the roof. With a start, I recognized the cathedral. It looked as quiet, dark, and still as every other place.

I gaped. "But why?"

The moon cast an illuminating glow on Kieran's face. He gestured at the sky. "It is a night of Power. Morrigu has been creeping about lately. Last night, I followed him."

"A night of what? You've been following him around by yourself?" My voice rose in exasperation.

"Power. A night of Power. Even in Lor, they must tell stories about the One's very lifeblood . . . that which gives life and energy to the Land . . . the Power. The storytellers say it is strongest on a full moon. And yes, I followed Morrigu last night."

"Why didn't you wake me?"

"I tried, but the thundering of your snores chased me away."

"I *don't* snore!"

Kieran rolled his eyes. The whites shone clearly, even in the dark. "It was easier for me to watch him in the Castle, all right? His bedchamber is just down the hall from mine. Anyhow, he came here last night and stayed inside for hours. He hardly seems like the praying type, so tonight, I hid inside the sanctuary to see what he was doing. Sure enough, he came again. And he wasn't inside for a moment before he opened a concealed door and disappeared into a tunnel. That's when I went to get you."

My head spun with questions, but I forced myself to put them aside for now. "All right, then. Let's get on with it."

We loped across the street, on the lookout for prying eyes, but no one seemed awake at this hour, not even the burrowing animals.

The cathedral's tall oaken doors did not even squeak as we opened them and slipped inside. During the day, the interior was awash in colors from a great

51

stained glass mural of Shaddai creating the mountains, seas, and animals. Now, though, we saw only huge, moving shadows from the lit candles atop the altar. I took one of the candelabra and held it for Kieran as he went straight to the back wall where massive, heavy tapestries hung. Drawing one aside, he felt along the wall's wood paneling, pushing until a click sounded and a hidden door opened outward, scraping along the stone floor.

The candles shone into a lightless void beyond. A tunnel.

Kieran's eyes met mine wordlessly. I stepped inside, feeling along the rough stone wall. Kieran followed a step behind me since I carried the light. The narrow tunnel extended only a little above our heads. Several times, I banged my head on low-hanging rock. The air here smelled musty and old, like a tomb. At every bend, I feared we might run directly into Morrigu.

The tunnel gradually became larger, opening until both of us could walk side by side. After a time, just to keep track, I counted my footsteps. At two hundred, a faint glow appeared ahead, coming from a room off the tunnel. Kieran leaned over and blew out the candles. Hunched and ready, we continued along until we came to the opening surrounded by a wide lip. We pressed ourselves against the cold stone on either side of the opening.

The room inside was huge, as large as the king's dining hall, and shrouded in darkness. It smelled like sulphur and smoke. A circle of pillars stood in the middle, dimly illuminated by three torches. Morrigu and the king stood within the pillar-circle, facing each other, and we could see and hear them clearly.

Shadows obscured the king's eyes and deepened the hollows in his cheeks.

"Here I am again, Morrigu, lured by your strange powers, seeking to know what you have hinted at during these many visits." An odd bitterness tinged the king's words.

"Tonight, you will see such wonders as you never dreamed," Morrigu assured him in a low, smooth voice. "So much that it may disturb you, though."

"I am not quite so blind as you would sometimes believe, my lord Morrigu. I have guessed at your true origins."

"Of course, Your Highness. This will not take long. The Power of the Land is strong tonight."

Morrigu let his head fall back. His arms hung loosely at his sides. Slowly, he began murmuring very low in a language I didn't recognize. Sweat beaded on my forehead and forearms as I watched. Morrigu's chants grew louder and stronger. His body swayed and his eyes screwed shut. The king watched with an absorbed expression.

The air around me felt strange—warm and charged, tickling the bare skin of my arms and face with tiny, invisible sparks. I clenched my fists to keep them from trembling and to center myself.

A startling crack split the air. Immediately, a glowing light sprang from Morrigu's fingertips and enveloped the king. The king threw his head back and his arms dropped limply to his sides. In the sudden flood of light, I saw Kieran's face, stark and tight. He moved forward. I flung myself at him and grabbed both of his arms, holding him back. The light surrounding King Rodell pulsed slowly, fading with each throb until it was merely a glow.

53

"Do not wait to test your powers. They will not last long," said Morrigu.

Rodell held out a hand toward one of the pillars surrounding him, fingers spread wide.

"Focus on the lines of Power all about you. You can feel them now if you try," Morrigu advised.

"I ... can," the king said in amazement. "They ring slightly–like the low tones of a bell."

"And how do they feel?"

"Hot ... burning!"

"Yes," hissed Morrigu, his face ghoulish in the torchlight. "Use them!"

The king's body tensed. I expelled a breath I didn't know I was holding, and at the same time, I released my hold on Kieran, who seemed to have calmed down. Neither of us could tear our eyes from the scene before us.

A low rumble sounded. "It's working!" the king cried.

It seemed to come from all around us. Kieran caught his breath. His eyes flicked to mine. The king gave a wild laugh.

A tremendous crack split the air. The pillar he pointed at exploded from within. Debris flew everywhere and dust billowed out to surround the king and Morrigu. When it cleared, the pillar lay in pieces all around them.

The king laughed again, grabbing onto Morrigu's shoulders in excitement. "It worked, just as you said!"

"That is only the beginning, my king. Soon, you will be able to tear down the buildings which house your enemies with nothing more than a thought. You will be able to look inside the minds of your counselors and know who is plotting against you. The

Power will allow you to tear out their hearts without getting a drop of blood on your doublet."

"But where is the fun in that?" the king asked, gleeful.

"Not just fun, my lord. Delight. Rapture. Transcendence. Together, we can make your wildest dreams come true."

The king sobered. "My wildest dreams. They come with a price, don't they?"

"Everything comes with a price, my king. Tonight, it is paid by the Land itself. By the Power that surges at this most sacred of times, the days surrounding the equinox."

"This will not last long, then."

"No. Not unless—"

"Do not tease me," the king commanded, all humor suddenly gone. "Speak plainly. What must I do to keep it?"

Morrigu chuckled, brazen in his defiance. "Why do you ask me? You already know. Perform the sacrifice on the night of the summer solstice and it will be yours. All this and more."

"Is there no other way?" The king no longer sounded angry.

Morrigu's voice sounded soft, almost gentle. "No, my king. The sacrifice should be made on the night of the summer solstice. Then your desire will come into being. I know the ways to make it so. Come again tomorrow, and we will prepare further."

He turned and left, heading toward the tunnel—and us. Instinctively, I pulled Kieran away from the opening, farther into the shadows. Morrigu paused just before the doorway. My heart hammered in dread. Then, in a flash of movement, he passed us.

The strange energy that had filled the space in heavy, invisible clouds evaporated all at once. The king stood alone next to the blasted pillar.

"Cruel," he whispered. "So cruel."

He slumped to the earth, head hanging and his breath coming in rasps.

We watched him for what seemed like a very long time, but he did not move. Finally, I tugged Kieran's arm, and together, we crept back down the tunnel. We went slowly in the suffocating darkness, feeling our way along the tunnel walls and listening for any sign of Morrigu ahead of us or the king behind us. At last, we reached the door to the cathedral.

Inside, it was empty and quiet. Kieran made his way to one of the benches at the front and sat heavily, dropping his head into his hands. I sat on the bench across from him, wiping nervous sweat off my neck, mind reeling with the strangeness I'd seen tonight. Shaddai . . . the childhood tales I'd heard of Moleck and evil sorcery sprang to mind. How I wished I could convince myself that they were still just tales.

Kieran raised his head and looked at me. "I don't understand what just happened."

"They are both in league with Moleck," I said, the truth sticking in my throat. Like Kieran, I didn't understand a lot of what I'd seen tonight, but that much seemed undeniable.

Kieran winced. "Are you sure?"

"I'm afraid so."

"Then you must know what Morrigu meant about the sacrifice."

I swallowed and looked aside. My heart, lodged in my throat, pounded loudly enough to wake the dead.

"Lance. I have to know."

My voice emerged from my throat in stark tones. "The most powerful sacrifice would be a blood relative. Specifically, a child. Your father means to kill you, Kieran."

Chapter Six

Leaning against the garden wall, I watched as the Castle guard patrolled back and forth, back and forth. Somewhere nearby, a cock crowed, welcoming the dawn. A heaviness born of fatigue anchored me to the wall. I straightened and focused on the sight ahead. As long as I was distracted or moving, I didn't feel like closing my eyes and drifting away.

When the night guardsman nearest me paused to take a leak into the rose bushes, I flew into action. Like an eel, I slithered around the corner and dashed up the outside stairs, moving with all the stealth I could. The front door didn't even creak on the hinges as I slipped inside.

A wide staircase led to the upper floors. Nearby, I could hear the chatter of servants and the clatter of kitchenware. One of the cleaning girls who seemed to be around all the time would surely catch me at any moment. No one did, however. Once on the second floor, I looked around in sudden panic. All the doors looked the same. I had only been up here once before, when Carter gave me a cursory tour. A bit of creeping about and some blind luck led me to what I hoped was Kieran's door. I opened it and rushed inside. In my haste, I knocked into the urn filled with Kieran's collection of staffs and wooden practice swords. It fell over with a crash, breaking apart on the marble flooring. Kieran sat on the edge of his bed with his back to me, lacing up his boots.

He didn't look up. Mildly, he said, "I will inform Carter that he must provide you with training exercises to improve your balance and coordination. You would make a pretty miserable assassin, Lance."

"Lucky for you that I'm not the person who has it in for you."

He froze, shoulders stiff.

Considering what we'd seen together last night, it wasn't the most diplomatic comment. "Er ... I mean ..."

He looked at me out of the corner of his eye. "I know what you mean," he said softly. "And I know why you're here."

I walked around the bed so that I could look him in the face. His blue Stormlifter eyes remained downcast.

"Please reconsider," I begged. "You're walking into the den of a very hungry lion."

"I know you think that I am. You're not exactly quiet about your convictions, you know.""Well, I'm on your guard in order to protect you, not watch as you get killed."

Now he did look up at me, and I felt the full measure of his gaze, intent and convicted. "I'm not going to get myself killed. He's my father, Lance. I can barely remember my mother. Her heritage lines are lost, and I don't even have them to comfort me. I must try to change his mind. He's all I have left of my family." The desperation in his voice rang through his quiet words. I could understand his desire despite myself. The ache of being an orphan was deep and familiar.

"Kieran, have a care for me if not yourself. Don't do this, please."

Kieran stood and stepped toward me. "He must have some measure of feeling left for me somewhere deep inside. Try to understand, Lance. I won't be able to live with myself if I don't try everything I possibly can to get through to him."

"Prince . . ." I said helplessly.

He looked at me sharply. I remembered to address him by his name instead of his title most of the time. But I had been a commoner a lot longer than a member of the prince's guard, and sometimes—all right, most times—it showed.

"Kieran. Do you have any idea how incredibly infuriating you can be?"

He flashed a weak smile. "Never let it be said that at least one of your personality attributes hasn't rubbed off on me. Now get back to the barrack before Carter suspects you're missing."

Damn it. Failure. Nevertheless, I tried to lighten my tone. "Oh, you know him. He'll yell at me one way or the other. It doesn't seem to matter about what."

Silence fell between us. After a moment, he rasped, "Humor me, then, and go."

I cleared my throat. "You . . . you're not alone, Kieran."

He looked at me, eyes bright, and nodded.

I left, heading down the staircase to the front door like I belonged here. No one bothered me, thank Shaddai.

How could I judge Kieran? I would have given anything to speak to my own true father, even if he turned out to be the vilest criminal in the Land, and even though it would bring pain to my adopted parents, who have done only good for me.

From here, I could see the pinnacle of the cathedral we had left so few hours ago. "Shaddai, protect him," I prayed. Then, after consideration, "Protect us all."

&

About an hour later, the other members of the prince's guard and I followed our charge into the stable. The summer solstice did not occur for another two days, so while I didn't like what Kieran was doing, it seemed that he had a little time yet.

The king stood illuminated in the circle of bright early light like a holy prophet, one hand on the pommel of his great black steed, head cocked as he murmured something low and private to his Morrigu. The two of them shared a laugh, the king's head thrown back, the bark of sound from his powerful throat booming off the rafters. Morrigu's hissing chokes joined his. If a snake could laugh, it would undoubtedly sound just like him.

When Kieran appeared, slim and grave, we guardsmen trailing him like a line of loyal hounds, the king's face transformed. The glow of humor evaporated, replaced at once with a darkened stillness, the sort of regard one might bestow on an insect.

"Father, may I accompany you on your ride?" Kieran asked in a clear voice.

King Rodell mounted his great ebony horse and looked down at Kieran, an imperious frown twisting his lips. Was it because of the request, or the title Kieran had given him? After a noticeable hesitation, he said, "Certainly. I desire privacy, however. Leave your guardsmen behind."

Kieran glanced at Morrigu, questioning. Morrigu's dark eyes glittered like stones worn smooth by the bottom of a rushing river. "Does your advisor accompany us?"

"Not today," answered the king. "Morrigu fears the cloudy sky. It might mess his fine silk shirt."

Morrigu snorted with amusement. Indeed, today, he wore an orange brocaded blouse and an indigo hat with a blood red plume that reminded me of a rooster's wattle.

A groom scurried to ready Goldie for Kieran. As he mounted, Kieran glanced at me. I read a thousand questions as well as apprehension in his eyes. Then, in a flash, he wheeled Goldie around and he and Rodell took off at a trot. At the sight of them, a cold feeling crowded my gut.

Morrigu turned on his heel and left the stable without a backward glance.

The other guardsmen and I stood looking at one another in the sudden silence. Carter said, "Back to the barracks with the lot of you. We've drills to do until they return."

Low groans and halfhearted protests filled the air.

Carter regarded me. "Except for you, young Lance. Fetch my boots from the cobbler's."

"Now?" I asked, craning my neck to watch Kieran as long as possible.

Laying both hands on my shoulders, he turned me around and pointed in the direction of the city. "Now. I wager the prince will be safe in the company of his father."

Several of the other guardsmen chuckled. Doubtless, they thought that everything was fine with their king and their world.

Carter arched one eyebrow at my hesitation.

I held up my hands in a gesture of surrender. "I'm going."

As soon as I was out of Carter's eyeshot, I ran down the clothier's row and zigzagged past vendors' tables, a flock of geese being herded by a comely lass, and two laborers quarreling over a broken shovel. I had nearly lost Morrigu already. He moved like a darting bird, veering this way and that on an unpredictable path.

Morrigu had appeared in Citadel a little more than a year ago, from what I had been able to discover. An obscure baron of an obscure land, he nevertheless had a sharp mind and clever ideas. The king, who had always admired those bold of spirit, saw the wisdom in his counsel. Soon, Morrigu had become Rodell's chief advisor.

I thought back to the first time I'd seen Morrigu and the sneer that twisted his lips when he looked at Kieran. I hadn't suspected him of true evil until last night. Perhaps his silly hat and fancy clothing had fooled me. Perhaps that had been his intent all along.

A bright blue and green parrot sat on the back of a placid black dog who walked next to a smiling shop proprietor.

"Morel the Magnificent!" the bird crowed. "The best carpets in the land!"

The shopkeeper gestured toward his store invitingly as I hurried past.

Morrigu seemed lost for a moment until I snatched a glimpse of the colorful feather of his hat down an alleyway. I hurried after him, emerging onto the street of metal workers. It looked somewhat familiar, but that didn't mean much. Six weeks was not enough time for me to get used to the bewildering warren of streets and alleys that coalesced into Citadel.

Sweating, I forced myself to slow down enough to peer into the shops. No luck. Then, in increasing panic, I hurried down an adjoining avenue before making my way back to the street of metal workers.

"Shaddai," I prayed, "favor your servant and reveal what the wicked would keep hidden."

Unfortunately, Shaddai gave me no immediate answer. A flash of memory distracted me. Now I remembered why this area seemed familiar. I had visited this very street to pick up my newly made chain mail. I walked a little farther north, where a distinctive red door frame marked the royal armorer's shop. I had taken no more than a step toward it when the door swung open. Some errant impulse made me duck behind a display of barrels rather than reveal myself. Thankfully so. Morrigu himself slipped out the door. What ...? He slithered off without a backward glance.

I waited a few breaths before entering the armorer's shop. The owner, Medwin, stood in all his beefy, sweaty glory next to a huge barrel of water, cooling a sword. Clouds of steam partially obscured his face. He broke into a wide, gap-toothed grin upon recognizing me.

"Young Lance! What brings you here? You're not having problems with the armor, are you?"

"No, no. Err . . . was that Lord Morrigu I saw leaving just now?"

Puzzlement wrinkled Medwin's wide brow. "Sure enough, you're right. 'Twas the lord himself. 'Twas the strangest thing. This *bam, bam, bam* on me door in the middle of the night! The wife was none too happy about that, let me tell you. She gets a fearsome temper when somebody wakes her up. Why, I've taken to creeping around like a little bunny rabbit in the evening lest I drop a pan or trip over a chair or—"

"Who was at the door?" I interrupted. I knew from prior experience with the verbose Medwin that the wife story could have gone on for quite some time. Plus, I had gotten a glimpse of his wife on my previous visit. Her grumpy expression and demanding snarl made me think that Medwin could have filled an entire hour with tales of her dislikes.

"Huh? Oh, yes. So, there was this *bam, bam, bam* on me door last night, and I get up—making sure to be quiet, you know—and who was it out the door? Lord

Morrigu! In the blackest heart of the night. Why, it must have been midnight or maybe later! 'I have a special job for you,' says he. 'Take one of your finished daggers and inscribe it with these designs.' Strange designs, they were! Oh, and it had to be finished by dawn. He paid me himself just now— double, if you believe it." He held up a sack of coins, smiling. Then he frowned of a sudden. "Say. . . he did say to be quiet about it. You'll keep it to yourself, won't you now, lad?"

An awful, sinking feeling came over me. Why would Morrigu need a special dagger finished today? A dagger with strange designs. I thought about the old stories of the Heathen Wars and the sorcerers who wielded rune-covered objects.

"Medwin!" I shouted, making the big man jump. Kneeling, I drew likenesses of the swirling, vine-like runes in the earthen floor. "Did the designs look like this?"

"Why, yes, they did! How did you know that?"

Shaddai! The dagger must be for a ritual . . . one to be performed this very day. Last night, Morrigu paused just outside the cave room. What if he somehow knew of our presence there and decided to proceed with the sacrifice sooner, rather than later? Heart thudding, I tried to force my stunned, sluggish brain to function.

Carter. Somehow, he would help me. I ran from the smithy's shop, leaving Medwin with dismay stamped across his broad face. My breath came short and harsh as I turned corners and dodged pedestrians. One name consumed my thoughts. Kieran.

I burst onto the practice field to find Carter under the barrack porch, talking to Marl and Uffen. He looked at me with annoyance when I ran up and gasped, "We must find the prince. He is in grave danger!"

Carter scowled. "What is this nonsense?"

"The king—Morrigu—Shaddai! No time to explain! Someone is trying to kill Kieran—now, as we speak!"

"You expect me to believe that wild-eyed notion?"

"I swear upon my life it's the truth! I'll explain as we ride. Please, Carter, it may already be too late."

Carter searched my eyes for what seemed like a long moment. Then he looked at the darkening sky. I could sense his thoughts. Did he want to listen to a puppy's hysterical barking and risk looking like a fool? Furthermore, a fool in a thunderstorm?

But I couldn't wait around to convince him. If I had to, I'd leave without him.

An instant later, Carter snapped, "If this is some kind of trick, I'll have you on the whipping post!" He gestured at Marl and Uffen. "Come with us."

I had no time for relief. We dashed to the stables. Carter barked questions to the boys there. No one knew the king's precise destination.

"The hills," Carter said after brief contemplation. "He prefers riding there."

In a flash, we mounted four horses and took off, riding out of the city gates.

My mount was a strong-legged black with a dark brown mane. His gait rolled with powerful intent as we thundered past merchants and other travelers heading into the city. They gaped at us. How recently I had been just like them, innocent and ignorant of royal plans and schemes.

Clouds hung dark and heavy above us. The wind rushing across my face smelled wet and thick. Before we'd crossed half of the valley, the first few splatters of rain poked at our faces and eyes. My mind sped on ahead faster than my horse could go. The crags and brush revealed nothing of Kieran and the king.

Carter shot me a dark look, but he must have seen the worry in my face because he just leaned into his horse and continued onward. The rain grew harder in scarcely a moment's time.

Lightning splintered the air ahead of us, followed by the tremendous crack of thunder. The thick smell of wet grass rose from our horses' hooves. At the edge of the valley, we halted our mounts at the top of a ridge. A rock outcropping lay to the right, and another gentle valley to the left.

"They could be anywhere!" Carter shouted over the wind. "Boy, come with me. Marl, Uffen, into the valley."

We were off again, Carter and me aiming for the rock outcropping. The grass was sparser here, but the ground had been chewed up by a prior storm and I couldn't discern any tracks. I kicked my mount on faster, threading my fingers deeper into his coarse mane. We rounded the outcropping. The breath tore from my horse's lungs like a bellows.

"Is that them?" Carter snapped, pointing up the rocky hill before us.

At the top of the hill, two figures faced one another beside the broken columns of some old structure. An ancient pagan temple, perhaps? I recognized Kieran's black doublet. With a great leap, I urged my horse forward.

Carter followed on my heels. Together, we scrambled up the steep hill, rife with slippery earth and sharp stones. At once, I seemed melded to the body of my horse. I felt his surefootedness and his great heart laboring within his chest. Near the top of the slope, my horse slipped and skidded down a good twenty feet.

"Again!" I ordered the animal.

He lunged forward as though responding to my command. Straining and heaving, this time, he climbed the top. Kieran and the king grappled ahead of me. I had no eyes for Carter, somewhere behind me. He cursed, and his horse grunted with effort. His horse must have floundered. I was now alone.

My horse stretched his legs into a flat-out run. With unreal quickness, the king ripped out his sword and flung himself at Kieran. Kieran staggered back in surprise, and the sword descended, cracking him in the temple. He fell to one knee, clearly dazed. The king struck at his head again, savagely, and this time, Kieran fell on his back and lay still.

Lightning jagged downward across the slate gray sky. Rodell hauled Kieran to a large, flat boulder nearby . . . an altar? The king pulled a gleaming blade from a sheath at his hip. He held the weapon to the sky, arms outstretched as if in supplication.

My mount ran full out. My heart beat like thunder against my tight chest. Thought dissolved in pure physical reaction. *Kieran.* He looked so lifeless! The distance closed between us. The king looked up, startled and angry, as I threw myself from my horse and collided with him. It was like hitting a marble column. We tumbled several feet from the boulder.

My head rang. I looked up to see the king rising across from me. Hair flew in a black stream around his distorted face. Waves of fury emanated from his dark eyes. He tossed aside his ceremonial dagger and ripped out the longsword he'd used to fell Kieran. Shaddai, but it looked wicked! I unsheathed my weapon, which suddenly seemed no bigger than a toothpick. I glanced around for Carter. Nowhere.

I didn't even have time to whisper a plea to Shaddai before the king attacked.

Immediately, he drove me back. I responded with all my strength, trying to mimic Carter's blunt style. The king smashed aside my efforts with two well-placed blows that made my sword ring.

I bit my lip and attacked, to little avail. The wind came off my back. While the king's hair blew away from his face, mine blinded me. Rodell struck a solid blow against my ribs, and pain drove the sight from my eyes for an instant. My vision cleared in time to see the king's sword descending in a move designed to split me in half. I flung myself aside.

The king attempted to follow my unexpected move and stumbled, cursing, into a nearby rock pillar. When he faced me again, his face showed ugly rage. Gripping his blade in both hands, he swung it at me. I brought my sword up to defend myself. Our blades connected with such force that my sword was jolted from my hands. It clattered against a rock, just out of reach.

I sprang to my feet, trying to circle around and pick up my weapon. Every time I reached for it, he swung, narrowly missing my fingers. He approached relentlessly, a smug look of victory on his face. The breath tore in and out of my lungs. I slipped on rain-slick rocks as I darted left, then right. The king effortlessly countered each move. This was my first real battle and, it seemed, my last.

A movement caught my eye. Kieran was leaning on the altar-rock, his fingers wrapped around the dagger his father had thrown aside. Blood ran down his temple, curiously bright against his deathly pale face.

"Father!" he bellowed. "Am I not the one you wish to kill? Why bother with my guardsman? Come, don't disappoint your dark god by denying him his sacrifice!"

The king's dark eyes flickered to Kieran. This brief distraction gave me time enough to jump at him and smash my fist into his jaw. He went down, and I followed, unbalanced by the fury of my attack. We wrestled, tearing and growling at one another. The king had the advantage of weight and strength, but I was young, quick, and resilient. I bloodied his nose and drove the air from his lungs with a knee to his abdomen. Both actions only enraged him more. He cuffed me on the jaw and knocked me backward onto the hard, rain-pelted ground.

In an instant, he leaped on top of me, closing his thick hands around my throat. Shaddai, but he was *strong!* I pulled at his hands uselessly. They were like iron. My head throbbed and the world darkened. From somewhere on the black, receding earth, I heard an agonized cry. The hands around my throat gave a convulsion. Then, the king's grip weakened and he fell half on and half off me. I choked for air.

When my vision cleared, I saw Kieran standing over me, his hands and head bloody, an expression of bleak horror on his face. I flailed, scrambling out from beneath the king's heavy, limp figure. His skull was bashed in. A bloody rock lay next to him.

"My prince!" Carter called.

A moment later, he had reached us. His face was grave testament to what he'd just witnessed. Kieran tore his eyes from his father and regarded Carter.

"The fate of our Land is in your hands. Will you be a truthful witness to Rodell's death?" Kieran's voice was strong and strangely dead. It cracked only once.

Carter stared at him. I couldn't discern his expression. He looked at the king's body.

"The old saying applies." Kieran's eyes were huge. "As the guard goes, so go the people."

"Yes," Carter acknowledged with a stone-like expression. "I witnessed his attack on you, and I witnessed his death."

Kieran touched his head in relief, then, and stumbled, the shock and his injuries getting the better of him. Carter caught him and held him steady as his shoulders shook and he gasped for air.

I noticed, after a while, that the rain was still falling.

.

Chapter Seven

We took the king's body back to Citadel, and I stood beside Kieran as Carter swore to the hastily assembled council that the king's death was justified. The news cast a pall on the city. Shops closed, women wailed, cathedral doors opened, and people crowded inside to pray for the king's soul.

Shar and Kenton escorted Kieran to his room. Carter pulled me aside. "The council will call each of us to explain what we saw. You'll not be mentioning the name of Moleck before them, youngling. Don't look surprised. I suspected as much, as I'm sure many of the council will as well. But you won't say the words, Lance. You were a child when the Heathen Wars went on. You don't know how panic spread through every household. The king is dead, and that is enough trouble for now. Understand?"

"Yes," I said, taken aback by Carter's grasp of the situation and by his presence of mind. "But—"

"No!" Carter said fiercely. "You *must* do as I say."

"As you say," I agreed. But I wasn't at all certain it was the right thing to do. What about Morrigu? Sly, sinister Morrigu, the instigator of this disaster. I couldn't just let him get away with this. Yet I did not know who he had on his side, and that could be dangerous for both Kieran and myself.

Not long after, Marl, Uffen and I appeared before the council. Morrigu sat at the head of the table, more somber and subdued than I had ever seen him, in a gray tunic and breeches.

Marl and Uffen testified to the king's increasingly erratic behavior in the preceding weeks—how he'd stalked about muttering to himself, how he'd order them to do something, then forget he'd said anything, how he'd talk to people who were dead and to those who didn't exist. I hadn't seen any of that, and I wondered cynically if they had or if Carter had merely instructed them to say that they had. When I went forth to testify, I told a carefully edited version of the truth—the king had seemed unstable the morning of his death, and that's why I had convinced Carter and the others to chase after him.

"Is there no other reason?" the head speaker, Marken, asked.

I looked directly at Morrigu. His eyes were black and narrow. He sat very still.

"None," I said, though the word burned in me. Morrigu was fluent in the game of politics. I'd not have him destroy Kieran because of my word.

He gave me a slight nod. I didn't acknowledge it.

As the day passed, I stayed just outside of Kieran's line of sight. He moved about with deliberation, weighing with extra consideration each decision he needed to make—what to wear for the funeral, which speaker should officiate, and which of the nobles would speak about the king. His face was a mask, his eyes like bright jewels, alive but fixed.

The guard stayed with him that night, in shifts of two. Kieran sat awake in the library, his hand clasped around a glass of wine someone had thrust on him. He was still like that when Marl and Uffen relieved Carter and me. I stumbled back to the barrack in utter and complete exhaustion.

Early the next morning, Carter shook me awake, unsmiling. "The prince is missing," he announced. "The others are looking for him. So will you."

Half awake, I wandered the streets for at least an hour before I realized that I knew precisely where Kieran had gone. I did my utmost not to think about just how I knew that. Instead, I navigated the bustling streets until one of them led me out Citadel's north gate and into the farm lands and hills beyond. I headed toward the nearest hill, grassy and forested with gnarled old oaks. At the top of the hill, I veered off the path toward a thick stand of trees, all the while telling myself that I was crazy to follow my instincts.

My instincts, it turned out, were entirely correct. Immediately, I found him, leaning up against a mossy old tree, looking out over the valley. Quietly, I drew near, but he seemed to sense my presence. He looked at me. Tears lined his pale face, still marked by Rodell's fists.

"I killed him," he said in a hoarse voice.

"I'm sorry," I replied, knowing that it had been for my sake and feeling guilty about the whole ugly affair.

He gestured at the valley, so green and wide and beautiful. "I would have waited for all this. Gladly."

"I know."

My words seemed to pain him. He turned his face into the rough tree bark and began to weep.

He was the king now, in every way that mattered, and his person was holy and sacred. Once, touching the king without invitation brought certain death. Still, I moved forward and gathered him in my arms. He dropped his head to my shoulder and clung to me like a child until the tortured shudders of grief subsided. We sat in silence for a while. Up here, the wind across the treetops sounded lonely and alive, strange and mournful.

"I must be king now," he said in a rough voice. "I must let the world settle across my shoulders. Despite everything, I want it. I do, but—"

"You're scared."

"Yes," he admitted. "Terrified."

I thought about mouthing some words of comfort, then decided to tell the truth. "You should be."

He looked at me, surprised.

I shrugged. "You'd be an idiot if you weren't."

He gave a little laugh, then scrubbed his palms across his eyes. "I must marry soon, as well. I wonder who my lords will foist upon me. A king must beget an heir. A king has responsibilities. He is the One's representative on earth, father to a people, an institution more than a man. Chained, locked, and bound, and all before my eighteenth birthday."

I thought of Shannon and the feel of her long blonde hair, the smell of her skin. "Some chains are thin and light."

He fell silent and then said earnestly, "Thank you, Lance."

It was pleasant there, on the hilltop, with the Land spread out all around us. We stayed for a little while longer in silence until it seemed to both of us that the time to leave had come.

We buried the king in a short and final service, conducted in a small side chapel off the main body of the cathedral, next to his ancestors and his queen. His body had been bathed and prepared with expensive oils and fragrant herbs, but the hard lines on his face remained, commanding even in death. Thousands of people lined the streets outside the cathedral, many of them from the towns immediately surrounding Citadel. The wailing they set up traveled in eddies and currents across the city like an eerie wind. Runners had been sent out to nearly every part of Cantwin after Carter had given the announcement that the king was dead. I saw no one from Lor since it was too far away. The outlying areas such as my hometown would hold ceremonies of their own to commemorate the rule of King Rodell.

The city awoke from grief into a flurry of activity the following day. Tomorrow, Kieran would be crowned king, and only one day remained to ready the Castle for the ceremony. What seemed like hundreds of people ran in and out of the Castle doors, carrying banners and decorations into the king's hall where the throne sat. Men rushed about, putting up tables and placing benches. Serving girls set the tables with freshly cut flowers in elaborate arrangements, silver and gold ware, and gold-rimmed plates and bowls big enough to drown a pig. Boys scattered flower petals on the floor and draped gauze over windows and doorways.

We in the guard brought in the meat—deer, pigs, and a mess of birds—and dressed them. Then, stinking and covered with blood, we descended on the bath house. When we returned to the Castle, tailors and servants hurried us into a large bedchamber and made us try on garment after garment. Clucking over the imperfections in the court wear, they measured and stitched and stabbed us with needles until Carter shouted at them to leave. Another group of servants then ushered us into a different room and began tedious lectures on proper deportment during the ceremony. And so it went.

A flurry of people—tailors, squires, nobles, and priests—surrounded Kieran as well. He submitted to their ministrations with an expression of patient resignation.

After a short night's sleep, we guardsmen were up again, planning for possible assassins and rabble rousers, stationing supplemental Castle guards here and there, sharpening our weapons, and drilling. When evening finally came and the nobles choked the halls, we shrugged into our prickly costumes and waited in the hallway, sweating and fidgeting, for at least an hour before the ceremony finally began.

Twelve smartly dressed heralds flung open the double doors and marched ahead of us, blowing silver horns. With Carter in the lead, the prince's guard strode down a long aisle, flanked by throngs of people, to the pedestal on which the throne sat. The Chief Speaker followed us and stood on the step above us, along with the Eldest Noble and several squires who held the royal crown, sword, and scepter on velvet pillows.

Carter had instructed me numerous times to keep my eyes straight ahead and my face expressionless. It was hard to do that and gawk at the gigantic hall at the same time. Gay banners hung from the ceiling in glorious colors, and the smell of roast meat wound its way through the crowd. Two groups of minstrels and a half-dozen court jesters waited against the walls for the celebration to begin. Glancing into the crowd, I noticed quick gazes and whispered exchanges directed at me. I was still a stranger here. Carter jabbed my ribs with his bony elbow, and I redoubled my efforts to appear stoic.

The heralds blared out a louder, more regal-sounding tune, and Kieran appeared, pale and handsome, to a general gasp. He wore the black, gold-embroidered mantle reserved for this occasion alone, a fine purple doublet, black breeches, and shiny black boots. The prince's sword, glittering with jewels, was strapped to his hip, and a gold circlet glinted through his dark hair. A large diamond sat atop the staff he carried as he strode down the aisle. We guardsmen drew our jeweled swords and crossed them, making a bridge for him to pass under.

Kieran looked neither left nor right as he walked. When he came to the steps beneath the throne, he knelt low and whispered a prayer before rising to stand before the Chief Speaker and the Eldest Noble,

Lord Banyn. Lord Banyn stepped forward and spoke to a silent crowd.

"Tonight, we proclaim Prince Kieran of the Stormlifter Dynasty, son of Rodell Courtenay, king over all the Land of Cantwin. Whereas Shaddai keeps us in peace and good favor, we ask that his priest bless this man before him now."

The Chief Speaker stepped forward, and Kieran knelt again. Smiling gently, the priest began a low, singsong chant while moving his hands over Kieran's bowed head. He reached into a bowl held by an assistant and sprinkled several drops of oil over Kieran's head and shoulders and then kissed him on the forehead. I thought of how the elders in my village had blessed me before I left on my journey. But how different were the circumstances! He stepped back and Kieran rose.

Lord Banyn continued by rote, "Is there any dispute over Kieran Courdenay's bloodline?" He waited barely a moment before saying, "Let the record show none."

"But there is a dispute, Lord." A voice called out from the crowd amidst gasps and whispers. A figure emerged from the rear of the room and traversed the aisle confidently.

Morrigu.

Lord Banyn sputtered angrily, "What is the meaning of this, Lord Morrigu?"

Kieran merely eyed his adversary grimly.

Morrigu held up a scroll. "Are we not a people of Shaddai, and thus a people of the Law?" His voice resounded in the hall.

"Of course, Lord Morrigu. What is your accusation?"

"I hold in my hand a writing of the Law, old, but still in effect." Morrigu unfurled the scroll and began to read aloud. "Any heir to the throne shall provide sufficient proof of his noble birth." Morrigu rolled up the scroll again and addressed the people. "We are sure of Rodell Courdenay's lineage, without a doubt. But what of Queen Shona?"

Kieran paled suddenly, and I remembered our conversation the other evening in his room. His mother's heritage lines were lost.

Morrigu, gloating and confident, extended the scroll. "By right of Law, I demand that you, Kieran Courdenay, produce proof of your mother's noble birth."

A collective gasp swept over the crowd. Kieran's tight face and silent lips told all. I stared with fury at Morrigu's rat-like face—so smug! What a pretty trap he had laid for Kieran. Pretty and deadly.

At last, Kieran said, "I require time."

"Of course," Morrigu said, suddenly magnanimous. "The Law gives you eighteen months. But at the end of that time, proof must be forthcoming. If it is not, your life is forfeit."

Shaddai! I think I may have exclaimed aloud, just like many around me. Rage, fiery and all-consuming, ignited a little-remembered fact in my mind.

I lurched forward. "I claim the right, as a loyal subject and sworn guardsman of my lord Kieran, to act as his champion!"

"Lance, no!" Kieran hissed.

I ignored him. "I will pay Kieran's penalty if proof of his right to the throne is not found within the allotted time."

Hatred, lightning quick and soul-deep, seared from Morrigu's eyes. The law, old and little used, was the stuff of bards' songs and children's tales. But it was still in effect, regardless. A moment later, Morrigu's ambition lay shuttered under an inscrutable stare.

"As you wish, Lance of Lor," Morrigu announced, making sure he proclaimed my bastard status to everyone. "You are the King's Champion. The task of producing Kieran's heritage records is yours, as is the penalty if you cannot. The office of regent, as held by Sire Banyn, is in effect for no more than eighteen months." He lowered his voice and sneered, "Shaddai's blessing to you, guardsman." With a swirl of his cape, he flung back his plumed head and strode out the main doors, leaving a swell of gasps and murmurs in his wake.

"What have you done, boy?" Carter, forgotten at my side, rasped.

In all truth, I didn't know. I glanced at Kieran. He stared at me, ashen-faced and angry. Shaddai. Queen Shona, the queen nobody knew anything about, the queen who died before she grew close to anyone at court. Realization of what I had just pledged bludgeoned me. I had done the right thing. I would do it again if necessary. But right then, I felt like throwing up.

By now, the entire crowd seemed intent on me, so I saluted and rushed blindly through the kitchen and out the back door. Once in the cool night air, I felt less nauseous, though my brain was still whirling around in a madman's dance.

I heard the muted roar of voices raised in scandal and outrage all the way out here. The knowledge that my name was on hundreds of lips made the queasiness intensify. A moment later, determined footsteps clicked toward me and Kieran crashed through the door.

"Damn it, Lance! What were you thinking? I will *not* let you do this," he snapped.

I took a deep breath before answering calmly. "You don't have a choice in the matter."

He stared at me, his dark face harsh in the moonlight. "Why?"

"Because I could. Because I wanted to. Because you deserve it."

"I deserve to fight my own battles! I deserve to have you here by my side as my friend and counselor, not halfway across the country, risking your life for my sake!"

"I'm not sorry."

Kieran glared at me in the dark for a moment longer, then sighed and leaned back against the wall next to me, his head tilted up at the starry expanse.

"I don't want you to die for me," he said with genuine emotion.

I smiled. "I'd rather avoid that fate myself."

Kieran's answering smile was small and strained. The past weeks had been difficult for him. "We must plan, Lance. We must decide how to proceed, how—"

"We must have a warm glass of wine," I said, taking his arm.

"A glass?" He guffawed. "Better a whole flagon!"

And that's just what we did, snatching one from the kitchen. We hid in the barrack, drinking and talking about trivial things. Kieran stumbled back to the Castle several hours later, quite drunk.

I lay down on my pallet and thought about home, and Shannon, and the long road in front of me.

In the morning, the city was unusually quiet. As I wandered through the streets looking for Carter, I quickly learned why. Several drunks sleeping on the streets made it clear that Kieran and I hadn't been the only people drinking too much last night. I found Carter sitting bleary-eyed in his kitchen, sipping a mug of tea while his wife fed their sweet-faced baby. When he saw me peering through the window, he scowled, but he motioned me inside. His wife looked at me, unsurprised.

"Oh," she said, "it's you. He's been complaining about you since last night." With that, she picked up their baby and left the room.

Carter gestured for me to sit down across from him at the solid oak table. The lines on his face were deep in the bright morning light.

"I need advice," I said.

He grunted. "You need a kick in the pants."

"Queen Shona . . . I don't know anything about her, and I don't know of anyone who does. I don't even know where to start looking."

He gave me a long, hard look. "I knew her. I was a youngster then, not much older than you are now. I remember when she and Rodell showed up here, Kieran but a babe in her arms. She kept to herself, silent and beautiful and somewhat sad. Rodell dominated the scene, and she let him. When Kieran was seven or eight, the plague took her. It was everywhere then. No family escaped it."

"And her heritage records?"

"They're not anywhere close by, I can tell you that much. Last night, after you decided to save the kingdom singlehandedly, I talked to the chief speaker. The churchmen could never locate Shona's records in the library here, and the king would never give them the authority to look elsewhere. You must understand that when Rodell first came, there was much unrest. The priests of Moleck constantly raided the outer lands, and King Elok the Usurper took more interest in his concubines than the government. When Rodell overthrew him and reclaimed his family's birthright, the people danced in the streets. He turned the country back from the brink of disaster. He saved us. No one wanted to challenge the legitimacy of a queen who hailed from a backwater northern dukedom, not after all Rodell had done. In any case, the speakers tell me that the records you seek are most likely in the library at Kesh, past the mountains."

I knew Kesh only as a faraway dot on a map. It lay past the Cantwin Mountains to the east in a land I knew nothing about.

Carter continued, "There may be found a large library that held many heritage records."

"Yes?" I exclaimed, excited. Perhaps I could even find evidence of my own origins.

Carter held up a finger. "Many heritage records *were* kept there until about fifteen years ago."

My excitement dwindled. "And then?"

"The Bel-Midron overran the city, slaughtered half the inhabitants, and burned most of the city. It's deserted now. The library may remain, though. No one knows because the area is still thick with those thieving nomads. Another thing—the champion traditionally goes alone. Don't ask me why—it's a stupid idea. You're as likely to die from that danger as anything else."

Carter got up and rummaged around the countertop for a few moments before returning to the table with a leather map. "You'll want to travel parallel to the Ribbon River until just after it forks into the Silver River, then through the Cantwin Pass to Kesh, which lies at the juncture of the Pardesh and Kesh Rivers. One or both may be dry at this time of year, however, depending on the snowfall earlier this winter. Keep to the back trails as much as possible. The way will be more difficult, but the chance of running across robbers will be less. I've told the kitchen to prepare rations for you, and the house servants are gathering other essentials . . . needles and medicines and such. They should be done by now."

I swallowed. "You think I should leave straight-way, then?" Somehow, I thought I'd have a bit more time to prepare.

"I don't think you should leave at all, young idiot, but since you've chosen this course for yourself, then yes, you must leave immediately. Kieran roused me out of bed before dawn, declaring his intention to accompany you on this quest. Don't let him. He's needed here."

"Yes," I agreed.

Of course he should remain, but I didn't relish the prospect of traveling alone again.

Carter gestured at a freshly baked loaf of bread on the countertop. "Hungry?"

I shook my head. We sat in silence for a moment longer.

"What are you waiting for? Gather your gear and be off with you before that fool prince finds you."

"Aye, sir." I rose. My legs were suddenly weak.

"Don't forget to oil your blade regularly. And work on the left-side block. You always leave yourself wide open to attack."

"Yes, sir." I suddenly felt shy and young. Shaddai, very young.

On my way out the door, Carter's gruff voice stopped me. "You may be an idiot, Lance, but you're a well-intentioned one. Shaddai go with you."

I couldn't help but smile. It was as sentimental as he would ever get.

"As with you, sir."

I gathered my meager gear and the supplies Carter had arranged for me, and without a word to anyone, I left the city.

Chapter Eight

Three days later, I stumbled along the rocky bank of the Ribbon River, having made my escape from Kieran and Citadel without incident. In an effort to follow Carter's advice to stay off the main thoroughfares, I had followed the river. My path had become increasingly rocky, and around the time I decided to head toward a more well-worn area, the vegetation became so thick that it forced me to continue slogging through the weed-choked riverbank, twisting my ankles this way and that nearly every time I stepped.

My boots wore ugly, stinging sores on my Achilles' tendons. My sword sheath, not made for long-distance walking, caused the sword's hilt to knock against the back of my head as I walked. The crossbow Carter had insisted I take seemed to weigh fifty pounds.

Yesterday at noon, the clouds broke and drenched me before I could scramble for cover. The rain soaked my woolen bedroll, making it three times heavier, and it wet my boots, which cracked and tightened when they dried. At dinner, I gagged down soggy bread and the last of the cheese. The thought of eating more of the water-logged bread kept me from eating yet today, and now, at noon, hunger complicated my other miseries.

All this wouldn't have been so bad if I'd had someone to listen to my complaints and distract me with conversation. But no. The champion goes alone. My mood worsened as I stumbled along until finally, fed up, I crashed through a particularly fierce tangle of scrub brush on a quest for a better path. In my haste, I scratched my face and arms and sent up a cloud of insects, several of which got sucked up my nostrils during an ill-timed inhalation. Huffing insects out of my nose, I staggered out of the brush and promptly tripped over a fallen log. As I fell to the ground, a shapely quartet of brown, hairy horse legs appeared before me.

"My, my, but don't you have a talent for dramatic entrances?"

I leaped to my feet, gaping. "Kieran?"

It *was* him, sitting atop his favorite horse, clean and dry, wearing a plain dark blue tunic and a big grin. He held the reins of another horse, a gray I recognized from the stables.

Curling his leg around the saddle pommel, he displayed smartly polished, tasseled boots and looked me up and down. "You're a mess. And you smell like moldy wool."

I swatted at the dust on my shoulders and picked bits of branches from my sleeves in an attempt to regain a little composure.

"*Mildewed* wool, perhaps. Nothing worse. Why are you here?" I squinted beyond him. He was alone. "Where are your guardsmen?"

Kieran unhooked his knee from the pommel and landed lightly on the ground.

"Who needs guardsmen? They only get in the way of all the fun, present company excepted."

"Well, you can't stay. You know that, don't you? I have enough to do without watching out for you."

"Watching out for *me*?" He guffawed. "Someone needs to watch out for you, my friend! I very kindly came equipped with food, wine, and dry blankets just for that purpose. Besides, Lance, have a care for my sanity. My kingdom has been taken over by a regent. What would you have me do? Learn needlepoint? Morrigu suspended my duties as prince as well when he challenged my birthright."

"Morrigu is the very reason you should stay! Shaddai knows what he'll be up to with you gone."

"Morrigu is crafty and power-hungry, of that I am certain. He may even want to take my crown. I think, though, that he's more interested in running the kingdom from behind the throne as he did with Rodell. This regency has tied his own hands as well as mine. The regent only has the power to conduct normal court affairs and settle petty disputes. In times of emergency, decisions are made by council vote. Even if the current regent meets an untimely demise, Lord Morrigu is too far down the line of succession to become the regent himself. Realistically, I have more to fear from one of my nobles, though none has the backing necessary to attempt a coup. I am safer here with you than within Morrigu's reach at home."

I grasped his implication after a moment. "You think he would try to kill you?"

"He has already tried once, through the king."

I thought I had left him safe in Citadel, surrounded by guardsmen. Guardsmen who did not like him . . . and who might be bribed.

"Don't look so worried, Lance. I do have some allies on the council and elsewhere. They will guard my interests and report to me, even while I'm trail bound."

"What good would that do you? You'll still be hundreds of miles away."

"My throne is as secure with me here as it is with me at home. Come, now, Lance, no more objections. I want to do this. I need to do it. I *must*—"

I put my hands to my ears. "Shaddai save me from the piteous howls of a princeling!" I cried, then paused as my good humor slipped away. "If you do this, there is no going back to the way things used to be. Not ever." We were leaving the boundaries of civilization, of life as we knew it, of the past.

"I know," he said with calmness, and commitment, and a gentle kind of strength that I envied.

The moment froze, stretched out in intensity and emotion. And then it snapped, and relief washed over me, and happiness, and a settled kind of joy. Truth be told, despite my blustering, I wanted him here.

Shaddai help me, but I *hated* traveling alone.

&

Sometimes, as I lay on my pallet in the barracks before exhaustion pulled me into its dark arms, a strange longing came over me. It pulled the corners of my soul apart so far that I thought it must tear. At first, I attributed it to homesickness. I missed the smell of Mother's baking and the feel of Shannon's lips and the sound of the wind sweeping over the fields. I even missed fighting with my brothers and my sisters' endless whining. But this was something deeper and wider than homesickness. It was familiar, too.

I had felt it before at dusk, when the light fell long and slanted and orange, or at night, when the cool sea air gushed through the open window. Once, in Lor, I had felt it when I stopped to rest at a maple tree after a hard day of threshing. I had laid my palm against the trunk of the tree, and a jolt of power, full and tingling, burst from it. Fleetingly, I saw strength and patience within the tracings of the deep, seeking roots beneath my feet. The experience felt natural and right. I realized, of a sudden, that the sensation had been with me for a long time, low and steady and real. I just hadn't acknowledged it before.

Now, on the trail with Kieran, the strange longings intensified. I had only to look toward the east, with its endless unfolding of shapes and colors, chasms and hills, to feel it. Perhaps it was only gratitude. How much difference a horse and a good traveling companion made!

Off and on, we walked the horses to save them from our weight and to stretch our cramped limbs. My horse was a fine tall gray with a white spotted rump, white mane and tail, and a glint in his round, dark eyes. Kieran couldn't recall his name, so I called him Silvereye after that glint.

As we went, Kieran asked about Lor. Once I started talking about it, I couldn't seem to stop. I told him about the hard work my father did as the town miller, the fights I had with my younger brothers, and the summer rains that flooded the fields one year and sent us scrambling for higher ground in fear of losing our homes. When my sister, Brenna, found out that we had left our old milk cow behind, she ran back to the house. She was pulling the cow through the mud when I caught up and hauled her away, kicking and screaming. I told him about my mother, smooth and round and jolly, and about the elders who read to us from the Law on Worship-Day.

I didn't speak about Shannon, though just thinking about her made a knot of want twist about in my gut. Neither did I tell Kieran about the bad times, like when an axe handle hit Father in the head and we didn't know if he would survive, or when little Curt wandered off for an entire night.

Kieran fell into a moody silence, and I suddenly regretted going on about my family when he had no family left. My thoughts must have shown up on my face, because Kieran said, "Rejoice in what you have, Lance. I always wished for the same: brothers and sisters and cousins. Anyone, really."

"What do you remember about your mother?"

"Just impressions—her warmth and her sweet voice. The king had a portrait of her hanging in his study. I used to look at it and imagine I remembered her long, dark hair and delicate hands. But I don't. She is hardly real at all anymore."

I understood his loneliness. Even though my adopted family loved me, they weren't my true blood, and I felt that loss always, everywhere.

"If she had lived, I doubt Rodell would have sent me to the northern lands for schooling. He knew that people in Citadel often distrusted those from the far reaches of Cantwin. Still, he kept me there for years, and when I returned home, it was not with parades and adoration, but in silence. And he was the one who assigned the guard to follow me around everywhere, like a helpless child." He sounded bitter.

"Don't think about it," I urged. "He wasn't always a bad man."

His jaw hard, he said, "No, Lance, I think you are wrong."

&

We navigated through chasms and hills, scrub brush and sycamore trees. Gnats, flies, doves, and squirrels were our only companions. We avoided traveling merchants and farmers and even clergy whenever we could. One morning, we topped a rise and saw a small village nestled up against a grove of cottonwood trees. Kieran nudged Goldie in the direction of the town.

"We don't need supplies. We should stay away from the villages as well as the main thoroughfares, just like Carter said," I chided.

"I know. And I know that we don't *need* supplies, but I haven't had a good meal for too many days and I want one now."

"Well, I really want to keep you safe. So we stay on our intended route."

He looked at the village, then back to me. "You're right. Unfortunately."

We plodded on for the next few miles. In the middle of crossing the Ribbon River, Kieran's horse, spooked by the glimmer of fish in the water, threw him into the cold water. She swam downstream for the better part of an hour before we could capture her. By that time, she'd managed to soak his packs, including the one that held the flour and spices. Back on the shore, Kieran dumped the sludgy mess onto the ground and looked dolefully at me. I looked dolefully back.

"Now we *do* need supplies," he said.

I frowned and held Kieran's gaze for a moment longer before sighing. "Very well. Let us return to the village."

Kieran gave a loud whoop of joy, and we both mounted our horses and took off back across the river.

We arrived in the village, Irin, two hours later, dirty, bedraggled and hungry. Our first stop was the bath house, where we soaked side by side in matching tubs until the water turned brown and cold. Kieran started a water fight then, and I jumped out of the tub and held his head under water in retaliation. He tried to do the same to me, resulting in a chase around the bath house, but he never succeeded. When the proprietor came in and harangued us for soaking the floor, we dressed in our second—and only—set of clothes, and Kieran pulled out a seemingly depthless pouch of coins to pay for our baths.

"What are you doing?" I yelped and snatched the bag from his hands.

"What?" he replied.

"If you let people know you have this much coin, you'll get both of us killed!"

"But—"

"But nothing!" I exclaimed. "I'll keep the money from now on. You are conspicuous enough already."

"What do you mean?" he asked, looking down at himself. He wore a peasant's gray tunic and black breeches and incongruous smooth, tasseled, black leather boots . . . boots far too well-made for any normal peasant to own.

I pointed at his footwear, and he grimaced. He had already heard me complain about them on more than one occasion.

"I can't go barefoot!" he protested.

"A peasant would be far more likely to go barefoot than wear those boots," I grumbled.

He looked at me with mock reproach. "You know, I think I liked you better when you first discovered my identity. You were too busy fawning over me to tell me what to do."

"You did an amazing job of curing me of that affliction," I stated happily.

After I paid the bathhouse proprietor, Kieran went off to find a washerwoman for our dirty clothes while I haggled mercilessly with a merchant for our flour and spices. We met again at the inn and ordered a pitcher of beer and two bowls of hearty stew. The aroma of the stew so distracted me that I nearly missed the young man sitting alone at a table near the door. He wore shabby, indistinct clothing and had a tousled thatch of dark hair that fell into blazing dark eyes. He didn't look away when I caught his eye, but instead rose from his table and headed toward us. "My lords," he said in a quiet voice.

Resisting the urge to groan out loud, I said instead, "You must be mistaken, young sir. We are not lords. My companion and I are merchants from Citadel, heading east for a visit with our families."

The young man gave a small, secret grin. He looked directly at Kieran. "I, too, hail from Citadel. I recognize you from there, my prince."

A chill ate at my stomach.

"You are mistaken," I said firmly, half-rising in my chair.

Kieran placed a calming hand on my arm.

"I understand your wish for secrecy, my lord. But I know who you are." He stared at Kieran, and Kieran, honest fool that he was, didn't repudiate him. "Shaddai bless you," the young man said, and he bowed slightly before exiting the inn.

We watched him go in silence, then looked at one another.

"I don't like it," I announced.

Kieran looked vaguely troubled, but he shrugged it off. "It's probably nothing."

"And if you're wrong?"

"Then I'm sure you'll let me know."

A fat waitress with ringlets in her hair delivered my stew. In between shoveling delicious spoonfuls in my mouth, I mumbled, "Let's just eat and go, all right?"

Kieran sipped the beer. He grinned. "The beer is cool from the cellar. It would be a shame to waste the whole pitcher."

Cool beer. Shaddai. When would we have a chance for that again?

We ended up staying almost an hour, and then we returned to the trail. Although we both kept vigil for the rest of the day, nothing out of the ordinary happened. Perhaps Kieran had been right all along.

The signs of civilization we had become accustomed to—the farms and villages and wandering peddlers—thinned out after we left Irin behind. The scrub brush gradually disappeared, leaving us to ride along rolling hills golden with wild wheat. Clouds shaped like mare's tails, long and thin and wispy, painted the sky. They came from the north, confirming that the weather would remain fair and warm. When we paused at the top of a small hill, with the earth spread out before us, Kieran said, "Beautiful," and smiled at me disarmingly.

A grove of dogwoods soon appeared, and near them, a stand of tall, nodding sunflowers. We stopped to peel and toast the seeds for a meal. When we started out again, we found ourselves back in meadows of wheat, picking through stalks as high as our horses' shoulders. Kieran rode in front of me, crushing a path and struggling with Goldie, who snorted and tossed her head, not liking the chaff drifting up her nose. I loved the smell of the wheat and the crackle it made as we passed through it.

An instant later, a different sound jarred me—wood bending and creaking . . . like a bow. I reacted quicker than I thought possible.

"Kieran!" I shouted. "Danger!"

I ducked close to Silvereye's spine as the telltale whistle of an arrow shot across my back, tugging at my clothing.

"Shaddai!" I yelped, flinging myself off my horse and yanking my sword out of its sheath. Kieran followed me an instant later. Our horses made broad targets and clumsy shields, so I swatted both hard on their backsides. They dashed off through the wheat breast by breast, creating a small trampled space in which we stood, looking about frantically for the source of the arrow.

Struggling to still my harsh breathing, I listened for our assailant. There—a quick curse, whispered low, perhaps a reaction to the fact that we were no longer easy targets. And then, the slow *swish-swish* as someone passed through the stalks of wheat toward us . . . no, not *someone*. Two people, light-footed and careful.

Kieran and I waited with our shoulders joined. I looked backward, he looked forward. Over my gulping, rapid breath, I pinpointed the direction of one assailant and waited in suspense for him to arrive. Still, shock hammered my gut when he emerged from the stalks, young and dark and far too self-possessed. He held a long, wicked blade. I recognized him—the dark-haired youth from Irin.

Damn.

Kieran's shoulder jerked against mine, and I glanced behind me to see another man facing him, this one tall, with a light complexion and a long blade that matched his partner's in sharpness and quality.

They jumped us in a soundless flash.

My practice sessions with Carter and the other guardsmen, long and strenuous as they had seemed, didn't prepare me for the desperate, brutal, lightning-quick struggle. I blocked every strike, stepping back and forward in a strange little dance. My opponent struck me as many times as I struck him. Sweat sprang from my forehead, back, and behind my knees. I smelled the sweat on him, too, full of sour fear. He was no raging madman like Rodell had been, but a skilled young assassin.

He hit me on the shoulder, hard. I jabbed the point of my blade into his leather-clad belly even harder. A whoosh of air left his lips, and he stumbled back. I crowded in. Reversing my sword, I struck a solid blow on his temple. The skin split and blood snaked into his eyes. His eyes crossed and he swayed. Shaddai! I knew I should take this opportunity to finish him with another solid blow, but I didn't want to kill him, restrained by all I had been taught about the sanctity of life. Then his eyes cleared and he lunged at me with a snarl. I hit the hard earth with a harder body on top of me. We grappled, both of us slick with sweat.

I managed to knee the assassin in the stomach. He fell, curling into a ball and gasping for air. I jumped onto all fours above him, like a lion straddling his prey, and swiped the blade across his exposed throat in a quick, terrible strike. His eyes went wide an instant before blood bloomed, bright red, in a deep swath across his throat. He thrashed, grabbing at his throat. I scrambled off his chest, watching in horror as blood plumed with every beat of his heart. He was dead. He just didn't know it yet.

Kieran and his opponent fought doggedly nearby, grunting with effort, neither making headway against the other. I got to my feet and drew up beside Kieran. The assassin's expression tightened. One of us he might best, but not two.

He reached inside his shirt, yanked on the great crystal rock hanging on a leather thong at his neck, and said a few words in a language I couldn't identify.

His eyes blazed, stark and large and angry, in his pale, tense face.

Something shivered through the air, like a heat wave or a sizzling fire brand . . . something invisible, but undeniably real. A sensation of danger overcame me, pulsing with Power, energy, and darkness.

"Come on!" I shouted to Kieran.

Seizing his arm, I dragged him backward through the tall wheat with all the strength I possessed. A half-dozen yards later, he stumbled, unbalanced by my frantic tugging. Tossing my sword aside, I flung myself over his body.

Light blazed from the man and the world exploded.

Tremendous pressure and heat seared my back, and a fearsome crack burst across my eardrums. Time slowed. I looked up to see smoking stalks of the wheat flattened in a circle. A red chunk of flesh hit the ground by my hand and broke apart, oozing blood.

I levered myself off Kieran. He sat up and looked about, hair mussed, cheek scraped, looking for all the world like a dazed, lost little boy.

Color was everywhere—blood, splattered bright red, turquoise skies, snow white clouds, and golden wheat waving in field after endless field.

Sudden, irrational anger took hold of me. I knotted my fists in Kieran's tunic and shook him with unnecessary force.

"I recognized one," I ground out. "The youth in the village who claimed to remember you from Citadel, who called you prince."

Kieran's eyes widened in comprehension. "He was making sure I was the right man. I didn't repudiate him."

"And by that action, you revealed yourself. It can never happen again, Kieran.

Swear me an oath. You must not reveal your identity to anyone until the crown is yours," I demanded, unaccountably and unreasonably.

He looked with puzzlement at my frenzy.

"Swear it," I persisted, possessed with the desire to keep him safe, to keep the Land safe through him.

He gripped my hand. "I swear it."

Sudden relief drained the anger away, leaving me trembling and weak. A moment later, I staggered into the wheat and became violently ill.

.

Chapter Nine

Two silent days passed. We hunted, traveled, cared for our mounts, ate and slept, just like usual. How silent the Land could be. Gentle wind, growing grass, circling hawks . . . all of them were blessedly quiet. I tried to lose myself in the silence and in the never-ending physical tasks our journey required. Kieran didn't make it easy.

"We're going to have to talk about it sooner or later," he said as we led our horses through marshland, trying—most often in vain—to avoid slipping on mud or stepping in slime-covered puddles.

"Then I choose later," I replied. I knew what he was talking about. How could I not? Exploding assassins. It's not like you see that every day.

"Lance," he said with a tinge of desperation. He had been remarkably patient.

I sighed and stepped across a decaying fallen log swarming with dragonflies. "Who do you think sent them? Morrigu? Or someone less obvious?"

"Morrigu, I think. Our unfortunate deaths would profit him. He has the funds to hire assassins, and presumably, the magical knowledge to show them how to explode at will."

"Then he'll try again?"

"Probably. But keep in mind that he'll have to find us first. He knows what we're after and can probably surmise what direction we're headed. He may even have his own agents looking for my records. For a while, though, I think we're safe. At the very least, several weeks. It will be that long before he realizes that his assassins failed. That's not what I want to talk about, however."

Shaddai. Something else?

"The promise?" I surmised, embarrassed about my panicked insistence.

He cast me a sidelong glance. "No, not that either. Right before my opponent burst into flames, I felt something—"

"Terror?" I interjected, hoping to forestall his questions. It didn't work.

"It was a sort of heat . . . no, that's not the right word. Power. A force. It seemed to come from you, just before the explosion."

I had felt it, too. "It came from the assassin. It must have."

"Some of it, perhaps. But not all. I'm certain that I sensed Power coming from you, Lance."

I frowned at him. "I'm just a peasant from nowhere, Kieran. Whatever you felt came from within you, not me. Think about the old stories. They tell about kings wielding tremendous Power to rain fire down upon enemies and call great winds to knock city walls down. Maybe you are a king in that fashion."

"Silly old myths . . . or so my—Rodell—told me. He would not abide tales of the old days." Kieran fell silent, deep in thought.

An idea occurred to me. Before he brooded himself into a deep depression, I quietly withdrew my sword and urged my horse forward a few steps. Very deliberately, I poked Goldie in the rump with the tip. Goldie squealed and jumped violently, causing Kieran to claw at her mane to stay in the saddle.

"Why did you do that?" Kieran cried.

I pointed ahead. Across a small field lay a bluff with a lone tree perched on top. "Race you to that tree."

"Lance, I'm really not in the mood—"

"I understand. You prefer to mope and mewl like a baby."

He scowled. "We'll see who will be mewling when I leave you in my dust!"

He kicked Goldie, and Silvereye sprang forward as well. I crouched low on Silvereye's back, the wind pushing back my hair and whistling through my teeth. Kieran cursed as I passed him.

I laughed, and Silvereye seemed to take power from my glee. He pumped his strong legs across the dry plains, sending up little clouds of dust with his strong hooves. He tired quickly, however, as the going was steadily uphill. When we arrived at the base of the bluff, both horses were laboring heavily.

Mindful of our mounts, Kieran challenged, "Take to your heels, if you can!"

I pulled Silvereye up abruptly, jumped off, and ran for the tree. Kieran followed suit, landing like a lean cat and scrambling after me. We raced up the hill and flung ourselves at the tree, hearts bursting. I won by a step, though it took all my strength. I didn't even have enough energy to gloat.

We lay there panting for a while, looking down at the horses, who were, in turn, staring up at us.

"They're too tired to make it up the hill," Kieran said. "Are you happy now?"

As a matter of fact, I was. Quite. "I merely saved them, and myself as well, from the excruciating boredom of your dark mood."

"Your consideration and thoughtfulness are boundless."

"I know."

He slapped me on the back of the head, then grimaced as his fingers came away wet with sweat. After a while, we dragged ourselves up to fetch the horses. Glancing over the hills, I pulled up short and grabbed Kieran's arm.

"Look! Is that a person?"

Straining our eyes, we stood staring at a distant hill to the west. A small black dot had been traveling down the slope, but now it was gone.

"Don't do this, Lance," Kieran said after a moment.

I regarded his serious face, confused.

"Don't start seeing shadows at every turn," Kieran said. "That will drive you crazy very shortly, and I've had my fill of crazy people in my life. I doubt very much if that is another assassin. On the slim chance it is, however, we will deal with the situation as it arises. Not before."

"But I'm sure I saw something!" I protested.

"You may have. Most likely, a merchant or some other traveling soul. We're not the only people in this part of the world."

"We should be," I grumbled.

He headed down the hill for the horses. I lingered there, staring at the distant hillside. Nothing. I shrugged and followed Kieran.

We walked the horses for the rest of the day, talking companionably. Eager to stave off both his melancholy and my discomfort over his observations about the assassins and the Power that supposedly flowed from me, I peppered him with questions about the One. Why did he refer to the deity by that name? Did he not believe that Shaddai had subdued the many gods at the beginning of time? Why else refer to him as the 'One'? How, then, if there were truly only One, as he argued, did he explain Moleck and other evil beings? And what was the nature of goodness and evil anyhow? I had long been curious about his beliefs, but I had held silent for fear of offending him. Now, though, I no longer restrained my curiosity.

"So many questions!" he exclaimed. "It's a good thing I spent the last ten years studying with monks!" He then held forth about their beliefs—the term, *Shaddai*, described a man-like god, not the wholeness of the divine being, with neither form nor formlessness. Therefore, he was the One. Shaddai did not subdue the other gods at the beginning of time, but rather, he encompassed them, even Moleck. As for the nature of good and evil, both forces resulted from the primal energies which created all life. And all death. This explanation confused me completely and kept me from asking further theological questions.

The day passed, and once again, we made camp. I built the fire to warm wine and the last of the meat we'd purchased in Irin while Kieran brushed and fed the horses, crooning softly in their ears.

After dinner, I sat staring into the warm orange flames and listening to the crickets sing in the dark. Kieran joined me, amusing himself by tossing pebbles into the fire. Not even a slight wind disturbed the calm night. The horses, whom Kieran had tied to tasty bushes, pricked their ears. Their reaction alarmed me. Father always said that animals were better listeners than people. Possible dangers revolved through my mind—bears, cougars, wolves, more creeping assassins—but instead, I saw a small white hand reach out from behind a bush and tug gently on Goldie's mane.

"Kieran!" I screamed.

Jumping up, I ran and launched myself into the foliage where the thief hid. I landed on an armload of branches and a squirming, foul-mouthed boy. With unexpected quickness, the boy nearly wrenched free of my grasp, but I got a firm grip on his wrists. Kieran picked up his kicking feet, and we dragged him into the light to see the contorted, enraged face of a child about ten summers old.

"Let go of me or I'll bite your ears off! I'll tear out your eyes and claw out your hair! I swear I will!" He gritted his teeth and snarled like a ravening animal, twisting back and forth with all his strength. His smudged face, long, greasy hair, and torn, filthy clothes made him look like an animal as well.

Kieran asked, "What was he doing, Lance?"

The boy immediately stopped snarling and snapped, "Lance? And what is your name, Black-hair? Spear? Arrow? Villain?"

"The little hell-spawn was trying to steal our horses," I replied.

"I was not!" he shrieked. "I only wanted to pet them!"

"While you were riding them away, you mean," I said.

This brought forth a long, strenuous volley of cursing. Kieran and I waited patiently until his face turned red and his insults slowed down.

"What is it that you do with thieves in Lor?" Kieran asked me.

"We strip them naked and tie them to a stake in the center of the village for three days." This wasn't exactly the truth, since I didn't remember anybody ever stealing anything as valuable as a horse before.

"Well, in Citadel, we chain thieves down in the dungeon where we let the rats feed on them." The touch of a grin hovered on Kieran's lips.

"But we have no dungeon here," I said.

"No village center either," Kieran observed.

The boy still glared at us, but his insults had quieted into mutters.

Sudden inspiration hit me. "I know! I'll make a spit and we'll roast him for dinner!"

The boy's flow of words stopped completely.

"I don't think he'd taste very good," Kieran noted, smoothing his chin in contemplation. "He's too scrawny."

"You're not going to hurt me!" the boy shouted.

"How do you know that?" Kieran asked in amusement.

This gave him pause. He contemplated. "Because if you wanted to hurt me, you would have done it by now."

Kieran looked at me. "He's found us out, Lance."

I released the little demon and dug through my pack until I found a coil of rope. He squirmed and twisted anew, but Kieran held him firm. I strung the thief's wrists together.

"What are you doing?" he wailed in outrage.

"We'd rather not have you loose to rob us while we sleep."

"You can't keep me here!"

"Why not?" Kieran asked. "Little boys should not be out alone in the dark. You *are* alone, aren't you?"

"Maybe," the kid hedged. "And don't call me a little boy!"

I grinned at Kieran, who returned the gesture. To the boy, I asked, "What is your name?"

He sneered. "Why should I tell you?"

"Because I'm going to call you 'Brat' unless you do."

"So be it," he said.

"Well, Brat, I'm Lance and this is Kieran. We just finished dinner. Are you hungry? Or thirsty? Brat? Brat, are you listening to me?"

"Paddy," he said sullenly.

"What?"

"Paddy, you dolt. My name."

"I never knew I was so good with children," I said.

"I'm not a child!" Paddy shrilled.

We propped Paddy up on a log next to the fire, and Kieran pulled out the remaining meat. Paddy's eyes lit hungrily, and Kieran began feeding him without a word. The child ate like a starving animal.

"Watch your fingers," I cautioned. Kieran met my eyes in brief concern.

Paddy noticed our gaze and slowed his pace down a little. He finished shortly and resumed glaring at us. Paddy was small, painfully thin, with dirty blond hair and a small, wide face. A thick layer of grime covered him like a second skin.

"Where is your family, Paddy?" Kieran asked softly.

"How should I know?" he snapped. "And why should I care?"

"They are your family!" I exclaimed.

"I don't like them," he said.

"What?" I stammered, flabbergasted. "How can you dislike your own family?"

"Because they don't like me either!"

I could understand that, given his abrasive personality. Kieran didn't believe him.

"I'm sure your mother and father love you."

Paddy glared at him. "Would you sell someone you love to Moleck's priests to be sacrificed?"

"They sold you?" I gasped.

"I don't want to talk about it!" he yelled.

I pitied the ragamuffin. What kind of family would do such a thing? No wonder he was so foul-tongued . . . if he was indeed telling the truth. I glanced at him. Who knew?

We fell silent, each of us exhausted by the recent struggle. Kieran sat back against his pack and suppressed a yawn. He was usually in bed before me.

"Sleep," I urged him. "I'll watch Paddy."

"You'll wake me when it's my turn?" he asked.

I nodded.

Kieran peeled off his dark blue tunic and rolled over in a blanket. Several moments later, his breath was deep and even.

"I can watch myself," Paddy muttered, glaring at me.

I tossed him an extra blanket and commanded, "Sleep."

He complied, but he did not sleep easily. I settled back and stared around at the night, noting shooting stars, the bow-man constellation, and the rustling of night rodents. The countryside here was devoid of villages, farms, hunting lodges and even hermits' caves, as far as I could tell. Paddy must have been on his own for days, if not more. He turned back and forth on his pallet, restless. Some time later, Kieran began mumbling and thrashing around in his dreams. He kicked his blanket off and, remaining asleep, cried out in anguish, "Father!"

Paddy sat up, glaring, his hair standing out in unruly tufts. "Isn't it enough that you're making me sleep with my wrists tied? Must I also listen to him all night long?"

"Be quiet," I snapped. "He's been through a lot."

I knelt by Kieran, tucking the blanket around his shoulders again.

Paddy continued scowling at me, but he didn't say anything. He lay back down.

I ended up drifting off to sleep on my watch. Kieran's hand on my shoulder awakened me sometime very late at night, when the fire had burned down to embers and even the crickets had quieted. I sat up in alarm. Paddy was still there, his blanket twisted around his legs and his head twisted to the side in a very uncomfortable-looking position.

"Some guardsman I make," I grumbled.

"Don't worry. It was a long day. I'll take over now. I'm having a hard time sleeping anyhow."

Though I felt ashamed for sleeping on guard, I didn't have enough energy to argue with him. I stretched out on my pallet and fell asleep in moments.

The sound of chirping birds and the smell of spiced tea woke me the next morning. I sat up groggily, and Kieran handed me a steaming cup. "This will warm your innards."

I took a sip and burned my tongue. Dew covered the rocks and grass and sparkled in tiny water drops hanging from the leaf tips of the nearby mulberry tree. Paddy lay sprawled out, still sleeping.

"What are we going to do with him?" I gestured at the little urchin.

Kieran sat on his haunches across from me. Dark half-circles shadowed his eyes. He looked at the boy with gentle concern. "He may be a thief, but I don't want to leave him on his own."

"Me either," I admitted.

Pulling out my knife, I leaned over and severed Paddy's bonds.

Awakening immediately, he sprang up, rubbing his wrists. He flexed his small dirty fingers and glared at us.

"They hurt!"

"They'll feel better soon," Kieran said. "Where are you headed?"

"Why should I tell you?" he sneered.

"Because if you're traveling in the same direction, you may want to accompany us," Kieran explained patiently.

Paddy squinted at us, then looked from the horses to the packs to the food. "All right. I'll go with you for a while."

"You will help," I added. "And if you steal anything, I'll hunt you down and make you sorry."

His eyebrows pulled together, but he nodded. I didn't think he liked me very much.

We tore down camp and headed out. I securely bound my belongings and kept a watchful eye on them. Paddy rode before me on Silvereye until I could no longer stand his stench. I got down and walked, and Kieran smiled at me knowingly. Paddy rode on, oblivious.

We went on for half the day, not talking. Clouds gathered in the east, by the far-off hills. At noon, we stopped at a stream. I glanced at Kieran, who read my thoughts precisely, and we both went for Paddy.

"What are you doing?" he shrieked, kicking and flailing.

"Sorry about this, Paddy, but if you're going to travel with us, you need to wash the Land off your body," Kieran explained.

He eyed the quickly approaching water hysterically. "I hate baths!"

"That is obvious!" I said.

We dunked him. Kieran held him by his skinny little legs, and I trapped his arms under one of my knees and scrubbed him with the spongy bristles of a plant that grew by the water's edge, clothes and all. Between the two of us, we managed to do away with most of Paddy's stench, though we both got soaked

114

in the process. Paddy's furious splutters and screams roughened his voice into a mere angry whisper by the end. When at last we released him, he waded out of the stream and stomped away. I half-expected him to roll in the dirt like a dog, but instead, he laid his ragged leather shirt out on a rock and sat next to it, waiting for it to dry and ignoring us.

"That was the most fun I've had in weeks," I announced, wiping water from my eyes.

"He'll probably try to stab us while we sleep," Kieran said.

We waded to the bank and sat, relaxing after the bathing ordeal.

"How much farther to Kesh?" Kieran asked after a moment.

I retrieved the map Carter had given me from the pocket inside my shirt, right next to my red flag, and laid it out on the sandy bank, tracing our route. "Probably ten more days, providing the weather holds. We'll cross the mountains at the Cantwin Pass. Is it familiar to you?"

"No. You?"

"No."

"Forgive me for asking, Lance, but how can we be certain that we're headed in the right direction? Your map isn't very detailed." Kieran pointed out.

I held the map out in front of me. True, it didn't include a lot of place names that I knew to exist, and I wasn't exactly certain which way was north, but I'd gauged our distance and direction by the stars as Father had taught me, and as far as I could tell, we were on the right track.

Paddy must have had remarkably good hearing, because he piped up, "You are heading toward

Cantwin Pass. Now stop talking so I can curse you in peace."

We left the stream and met a caravan of traders heading toward Citadel with their wares. Kieran restocked our food supplies and bought a new set of clothing for Paddy. I had since returned his purse to him—worrying about losing it bothered me constantly.

When the traders were out of range, Paddy threw the clothes in the dirt and snapped, "I don't need charity, Black-head." He stalked off.

Angered at his refusal of Kieran's generosity, I followed Paddy and grabbed him by the ear, twisting it.

"Oww! What are you doing?" he cried.

"Go back there and thank him for those clothes, and then put them on," I hissed.

"I'm not throwing away these leathers! My mother made them for me!"

"Then keep them to wear later, but do as I say," I insisted. By Shaddai, but he *would* learn some manners.

I released him and he stomped back to Kieran, turning and glaring at me several times over his shoulder. He shook the dirt off the clothing and in an astonishingly civil tone, said, "Thank you, Kieran." Then the immodest little fellow stripped and changed right there in front of us. I came up behind him as he pulled the tunic over his head.

"Wait." Pulling the tunic up, I examined an ugly scar on his back, below the shoulder blade. The edges were red and puckered, as if it had just healed.

I turned him so that Kieran could see. "How did this happen?"

Paddy didn't answer. I dropped his shirt and put my hand on his bony little shoulder, suddenly regretting my earlier harshness. "Did someone do this to you?"

"Yes!" he said, a murderous fire lighting his eyes. "And I'll kill him for it!"

I looked at Kieran over Paddy's head and read the same concern there.

"Come on," Kieran said to Paddy. "We've stayed long enough. You can ride in front of me now."

We mounted our horses again and took off across a patch of clover near a trickling stream. After we had been riding for a quarter of an hour or so, Paddy said to Kieran, "That was a heavy bag of gold you drew from to pay the merchants. Are you a nobleman?"

I could see Kieran resist the impulse to look at me. "Yes, I suppose you could say that."

"You *suppose*?" Paddy asked suspiciously.

"I must obtain my heritage records from Kesh first."

"Ah." Paddy turned to me. "Then what are you doing along?"

"We have a common purpose." It was a shade of the truth, if not the whole thing. "And we are comrades."

"I see," Paddy said, though he didn't seem fully convinced. His uncanny intelligence annoyed me.

"And why are you here?" I asked bluntly.

He thrust his chin up in the air and ignored me. Kieran tried a gentler approach.

"Please, Paddy, you must be from somewhere around here."

"Yes, I am," he replied, then he clamped his mouth shut tighter than storm shutters in winter.

"Give it up, Lance. We'll get no more from him today," Kieran said.

His words sounded strange, hollow and echoing. I didn't ask myself why, though, too overcome with anger.

"Ah, but I'd love to keep trying," I replied vengefully.

"What?" Paddy asked, looking at me like I was a complete idiot.

"I answered Kieran, you little nitwit."

"Kieran was talking to me, not you, and I answered him, you *big* nitwit."

I narrowed my eyes at him. "Kieran said, 'Give it up, Lance.' That's *my* name, remember? And if you call me a nitwit again, you'll regret it."

Paddy opened his mouth to screech some annoying reply when Kieran said quietly, "He's right, Lance. I didn't say anything. I was only thinking—" Kieran stopped short, his face paling. We regarded each other in shocked disbelief. Paddy looked at the both of us as though we were insane.

I turned and stared ahead at an upcoming stand of cedar trees. "I'm hearing things, I suppose," I commented firmly, and no one else cared to mention the matter again that day.

Chapter Ten

The following day, when we camped at dinnertime, I picked nearby blackberries while Paddy gathered firewood. He turned out to be a better traveling companion than I had expected, even though he constantly squirmed in the saddle, ate twice his share, and tugged on Goldie's ears until she turned around and bit him.

"Yow!" he screamed from the brush. He hopped around, pounding on his chest, under his arms, and behind his neck.

I threw a handful of blackberries aside and ran over to him, shouting, "What is it?"

"It ran up my shirt!" He thumped and whacked at his chest in panic.

"What?" I cried. I tried to imagine the poisonous creature capable of causing such a commotion.

"It's huge! And hairy!" He shuddered. "And black!" He smashed something under his shirt. "Die, spider!"

"A spider probably won't kill you, you little idiot," I said, helping him as he struggled to pull his tunic off. The spider, which was indeed very large, very hairy, and very black, hung, smashed and oozing, from his left nipple.

Upon seeing it, Paddy shrieked, "Eww!"

He ran straight at Kieran, who was hauling a bucket of fresh water from the creek. Grabbing the bucket, Paddy frantically splashed water on himself until he cleaned away every last bit of spider.

It was the only time he'd bathed without prodding from Kieran or myself.

We traveled onward for two more days along a series of ravines, falling into a routine. Kieran set up camp and cooked, Paddy gathered firewood and brushed the horses, and I hunted and gathered edible roots. We met no one, and I preferred it that way.

The fourth day was like the others except that the mild weather turned stiflingly warm. Around noon, I drowsed in my saddle. As I traveled between the land of sleep and wakefulness, a strange vision came to me. I sensed the Land about me, pulsing with life and running with lines of Power that spiked upward into rocks and mountains and plants and flared around deer and foxes, wild ponies and village dwellers. The Power, a fretful, living being, gathered with fast-moving intensity, growing so large that it must explode—

A flurry of crows burst from a nearby tree, cawing raucously, and jolted me out of the half-sleep with a galloping heart and a choked cry.

"Something wrong?" Kieran inquired, appearing puzzled at my panicked disorientation.

I looked about, and the world seemed clearer than usual, the horses and bushes and rolling clouds more detailed . . . brighter, somehow. I shut my eyes to steady myself, and I recognized smells with the same unusual clarity. Sagebrush, leather, horses, bratty little boys . . .

A hand on my shoulder and a concerned voice. "Lance? Are you well?" Kieran asked.

I rallied and opened my eyes. "I'm fine." Then, seeing the look of doubt on his face, said, "Really."

Then it hit.

A deep, rumbling sound came from the bowels of the earth, and the ground began to shake. Silvereye screamed in fear and reared up. I toppled off his back, and Paddy fell on top of me. The ground rolled and bucked like a half-wild border pony. Paddy dug his nails into my arms and buried his head in my chest. I barely noticed. Trees wobbled back and forth, and beside me, the earth split into a crevice several feet deep. Kieran struggled to control Goldie, who pranced back and forth, her eyes rolling with fear. When the ground opened another crevice near the panicked horse, she tripped and went down. Kieran tumbled off her back and rolled a few feet before lying still.

I hauled myself onto all fours and tried to crawl to him, but Paddy's weight and the unsteady earth kept me from going more than a few feet. At last, the rumbling faded and the vibrations ceased. I disentangled myself from Paddy's fearful embrace and rushed to Kieran's side.

Grasping him by the shoulders, I pulled him up to a sitting position. He groaned, dazed, his eyes fluttering, uncomprehending. Then, a moment later, his gaze cleared and a look bright with surprise and wonder transformed his face. He seemed about to say something, then restrained himself. Instead, he swallowed and asked, "Is everyone all right?"

I nodded.

"The horses?"

Silvereye was fine, though still nervous. I looked around for Goldie and saw her limping toward us. Kieran swore and got up to run his hand over the leg she favored.

"Is it broken?"

"No. I think it's sprained. It's already beginning to swell. We won't be riding her for a while."

Paddy appeared at our sides, his hair mussed and his hands shaking. "I know of an herb that will help. Father taught me. I'll find it." He ran off before we could stop him.

"Be careful," I called after him.

In silence, we went about setting up camp, unloading the horses and building a fire. When Paddy came back with the herb, I ground it up with a pestle and mixed it with mud and a little water before smearing it over Goldie's leg. Kieran bound it gently with a long strip of cloth.

Paddy whittled with Kieran's knife while Kieran began our meal and I cleaned the wounds on my arms made by Paddy's dirty fingernails. Infection from the little urchin would probably kill me. While the food cooked, I challenged Kieran to a sword duel, and we spent the afternoon hacking away at each other, Paddy cheering us on. I hadn't realized how much I missed sparring.

Afterward, when we were both relaxing pleasantly exhausted against our saddles and Paddy chased a butterfly around the fringes of the camp, intent on killing it, Kieran said softly, "Something is strange about us. I know that you feel it, too."

Shaddai. Here it came. I tried to avoid the subject. "We're strange, all right. A renegade prince and a bastard seeking a name. We're cause to make people stop and wonder."

Kieran ignored my jest, his face grave. "Don't deny the coincidences—the assassin, the way you picked up my thoughts, this earthquake. You don't want to admit it. I understand that you're frightened, but that doesn't change the fact that this strangeness—this Power—exists."

His words turned my stomach. I frowned at him. The late afternoon sunlight highlighted his face and illuminated his blue-gray eyes so that they suddenly seemed clear and mystical. He spoke the truth . . . at times, I did feel something strange and powerful, throbbing with life and purpose, at the edge of my thoughts. There was no regularity about it, no consistency, and no easy explanation. For all those reasons, I did not want to admit it. And the fear, as well. I could no longer deny the fear.

Kieran continued, struggling with the words. He was not altogether comfortable with this either, but at least he had the courage to bring it to the surface. "After the earthquake, when you grasped my shoulders, I *felt* your concern, as if you and I were one person, but separate. It is hard to explain. I felt your heart beating, your blood rushing, your anxiety that I was hurt. I think I could have seen through your eyes if I wanted to. Then I opened my eyes, and we were separate again."

His words chilled me. If he felt all that I had, even for an instant, could he then read my thoughts, as Shaddai did? The idea unwound me. Shaddai was spirit, holy and perfect . . . but Kieran? He was only a man. A king, to be sure, but still a man.

He must have read my mind in my face. "I'm not supernatural, Lance. I cannot hear your thoughts, if that concerns you."

Odd that he would voice my deepest concerns. I looked at Paddy, blissfully dashing after the butterfly, an innocent child.

"Sometimes, the earth around me is thick with Power," I said. "Invisible Power, but strong and hot—alive and wild. I feel as though I can grasp it between my two hands and work it. That I *must* work it. Except that I don't know how." I looked at him, embarrassed by my frank confession. "I don't know what I am saying. It is madness."

Kieran's unlined face was quiet and accepting. I had expected him to mock me, even though some deeper part of me knew that he would never do that.

"Perhaps," he said, glancing, too, at Paddy. The world about us blazed with the dying colors of dusk. "Perhaps not."

We couldn't ride Goldie for the next few days, nor could we walk her very far. We took turns riding Silvereye, and each of us grew bored and listless.

Kieran stepped into a gopher hole and twisted his knee on the second day after the earthquake. He then rode Silvereye exclusively. By the third day, we had run out of food.

Hunting back home on the Golden Hills was much different than hunting on the tree-covered foothills of a mountain. I wasted half a day attempting to creep around silently through a profusion of undergrowth that made it hard to see twenty feet ahead, much less spot a well-camouflaged animal. Nevertheless, I managed to make it back to camp with two rabbits. My efforts disgusted Paddy.

"This is all you came back with? Two scrawny little bunnies?" he jeered.

"I suppose you can do better." I was hot, hungry and annoyed.

"Yes, I can," he boasted.

He saw me roll my eyes, and his little face turned red.

"I'll wager I can find us a fat buck tomorrow with no trouble at all," he cried.

"You'll wager, eh? And what do you want *if* you win?"

Paddy's face twisted as he considered the question. "A few of Kieran's gold coins," he decided.

"Gold coins!" I exclaimed, amazed at his gall. "Isn't it enough that we feed and protect you?"

"No."

I grimaced and looked at Kieran. He was rubbing his knee in evident pain. "Very well." He scowled. "I will give you two coins if you succeed."

"And if you lose, I'll paddle your hind-end," I volunteered cheerily.

Paddy regarded me with disgust and went off to sharpen the knife Kieran had given him. I broke out laughing. Kieran mustered a weak smile. We sat side by side on a petrified log, silent for a long time. Finally, I said, "There's more on your mind than your knee."

My words roused him from a daze. "Just wondering what we'll find at Kesh."

I shrugged. "We'll find what we need. I'm sure of it."

He regarded me from the side, his mouth quirked in a wry, familiar smile. "Do you never doubt?"

"Doubt? Me? With my mighty sword arm and Shaddai overhead, why should I doubt?"

Kieran snorted. He rested his elbows on his knees and hung his head. "You're right. I'm being foolish. Sometimes, my stomach wraps around itself with worry. There is only one thing that soothes it."

"Oh?" I asked, since he evidently wanted me to.

"Music."

"Ah, music. Well, I've never been particularly gifted, but I'll sing a tune for you if you wish." With that, I opened my mouth and belted out the off-tune beginning of a bawdy harvest song. Kieran winced and covered his ears with his hands.

"Enough! Let me demonstrate what music really is." With that, he got up and rummaged around in his packs to produce his lyre. He ran his hand along the lyre's curved, polished wood with affection. I remembered him playing so beautifully during my illness, or had I hallucinated it? I sat back and made myself comfortable.

He plinked a few strings, twisted knobs here and there, and listened to the tones, studying the instrument by the light of the dying sunset. Paddy looked up, curious. Kieran closed his eyes and struck the first few chords with thin, lithe fingers. The song started with gentle tones, flowing and falling like rain. I knew, then, that I hadn't been hallucinating the night of my illness. He sat hunched over, his face rapt with the melody. Magic flowed from his fingertips. Mere wood, string, and varnish did not make up the lyre, but living passion and purpose.

The strains rose high and fell low. I thought of an eagle in flight over a lonely, faraway valley. A lone note wove throughout the song, swelling with longing, clear and crisp and brilliant. It came from Kieran's soul, filled with loneliness and love like the overflowing streams. He played on for a long time, until the sun set fully and the logs on the fire burned low.

I hadn't moved to feed the fire for fear that I would disturb him. Paddy had long since moved to the fireside and sat watching Kieran's dancing fingers in unrestrained awe. Finally, far too soon, Kieran ended on a gentle note and set his lyre down. He massaged his fingers. Looking up at Paddy and me, he seemed relaxed now, though exhausted. The night sounded strangely dead, as if it held its breath waiting for him to resume his song.

I groped for words, but they all seemed inadequate. At last, I settled for, "That was beautiful. You are truly gifted."

Kieran looked down at the ground, looking embarrassed. "Thank you." He got up and replaced the lyre in his pack, then lay down on his blanket. "Wake me for my watch."

He fell asleep in moments with Paddy and me still gaping at him. Paddy looked me in the eye and breathed, "What manner of man is he?"

I could not say it aloud, but I had only one reply. A king. A true king, our only king, gifted by Shaddai in all ways.

Chapter Eleven

We reached the Cantwin Pass two days later. Rocky crags jutted high into the sky, grass dotted the slopes, and pure white snow capped the peaks. I had never seen anything so beautiful. And so disappointing. What had once been the Cantwin Pass was now a pile of shale and rock splinters hundreds of feet high.

"The earthquake," Kieran said.

I stared stupidly at the pass, unable to make any such observation. Paddy's face turned red, and he jumped up and down in frustration.

"We're not meant to go this way, it seems," Kieran said.

"We could try to scale it," I suggested weakly.

"With our horses and supplies and the young one?" Kieran spoke in a low tone for Paddy's sake.

"We have to get to the other side somehow. We can't climb over the top of the mountains."

"Maybe we can," Kieran mused. "At university, I learned about a tribe of mountain people who—"

"Forget it," Paddy snapped, displaying an uncanny aptitude for eavesdropping. "Even if we didn't plunge to our deaths, the cold would kill us."

I took the worn leather map out of my pocket and laid it out for all of us to see.

"The next nearest pass is two hundred miles north!" Kieran exclaimed.

We looked at each other in dread. Paddy squatted down between us. "It's not marked here, but there is a pass about fifty miles further south. The man I learned about it from warned me that the way is hard and the Land there is filled with strange people."

"What kind of strange people?" I inquired.

"Superstitious ones who don't aid travelers."

That didn't sound so bad. Kieran thought so, too.

"It seems like our only option. We'll just have to be careful."

We turned and followed the mountain range southward. The rocky, uneven ground and whipping winds made travel difficult. Cascading runoff produced ice-cold waterfalls that often blocked our path, forcing us to pick our way across their streams. At noon, we stopped by one of the waterfalls to drink and rest. None of us had any stamina here so close to heaven.

Paddy ran off into the bushes without comment. I assumed he went to relieve himself. When he didn't come back in a reasonable amount of time, Kieran and I set out to look for him. A quarter of an hour later, we found him dragging a gutted buck on the pine needles behind him, huffing and puffing. His face broke into a huge grin when he saw us.

"You lose!" he wheezed, jabbing a dirty little finger at me.

I'd forgotten about our deal. Roaring in mock rage, I lunged for him. He screeched and ran away, and we chased each other in circles. Finally, I fell on Paddy and tickled him until he begged for mercy.

We hauled the buck back to camp. After exacting his coins from Kieran, Paddy insisted on supervising the roasting of the meat in herbs. He badgered me until I admitted that it was the best-tasting meal we'd had since leaving Citadel. Paddy crowed about his hunting and cooking skills for hours afterward as we sat around smoking, drying, and packing the meat for transport.

Rain fell every afternoon for the next week, light and cool, and after a few days, predictable and bothersome. Most mornings, we woke to a fog that moved snakelike through the trees. Game was plentiful—antelope, deer, bears, and mountain cats. We didn't spot the last two, but we saw their tracks and droppings everywhere. We ate well but didn't travel far. I spent my free time fashioning Paddy a new pair of boots from the buck's hide. Paddy helped me stitch them together, evidently pleased to discard his old boots, which had become so small for him that his big toes peeked out of matching holes.

One day, as we walked our mounts up a grassy slope under a cloud-speckled sky, Paddy commented, "At home, the peach trees will be ready for harvesting."

This detail of his home life surprised me and reminded me of mine. The thought made me grin.

Paddy, walking next to me, saw my smile and sneered, "Missing home, Lance? Do you have a girl there?"

I didn't have Shannon, and I probably never would, so I sneered back, "At least I know what to do with one!"

Paddy stuck his tongue out at me and stomped ahead of us.

Without the slightest warning, a blinding flash of lightning struck the earth not ten paces in front of him. Paddy flew backward, landing on his buttocks with a great, "Oof!"

The weeds around the lightning strike caught fire. I ripped off my tunic and beat at the flames while Kieran knelt beside Paddy. Paddy's hair stood on end and his face was very pale. He looked at Kieran in an uncomprehending daze. Kieran slapped his cheeks lightly, and Paddy came out of the daze with a start.

I joined them. "Are you burned?"

"Huh?" Paddy replied.

Kieran and I pulled up his sleeves and the cuffs of his breeches, but the little devil was unmarked. He pushed our hands away and snapped, "I'm fine!"

We stood around, looking at each other.

"Well," I commented, "*that's* never happened to me before."

Recovering his usual attitude, Paddy informed me snidely, "A mountain storm is coming. A big one, I think. They sometimes start with lightning."

"The pass," I said to no one in particular. "Will we be through it before the storm breaks?"

"Doubtful," Kieran said. "But we must try."

We started off again, doubling our pace. Paddy stumbled several times, his legs wobbly from the lightning scare. Without a word, I hefted him onto Silvereye. He surprised me by not protesting.

By mid-afternoon, the sky was black and lightning flashed nearby, chased by deep, thunderous booms. Cold wind forced Kieran and me to don our cloaks. Kieran also wrapped a blanket around Paddy's shoulders. We trudged on, and Paddy huddled into Silvereye's mane. My ears burned from the wind and my fingers stiffened around Silvereye's reins.

The rain began then, soaking our clothes and driving pinpricks into our faces. I held Paddy close for warmth. The icy rain soaked our thick clothing and made it difficult to see ten paces in front of us. Paddy needed shelter. I searched the bald rock face and scrubby pine trees in vain.

Sometime later, Kieran nudged my arm and pointed ahead of us—the pass. Paddy had called it dangerous. He should have called it insane. The pass lay through a steep fold between the mountains, the sides covered with unstable gravel. A brown, frothing river raged at the bottom. Getting to the bottom required a careful day's worth of travel, and that in full sunlight. Kieran regarded me with an expression of faint hope. I had none to offer him. Instead, I shouted over the din, "We need shelter!"

"Look!" He cried, pointing.

Down the mountain, I saw a cabin obscured by pines and lodged carefully on the curve of the mountain. A brief doubt crossed my mind. What if the cabin housed those that Paddy warned us about? One look at the boy hugging Silvereye's neck in misery made me decide to take the risk.

We sloshed toward the cabin. As we descended a small knoll, we saw a dozen or more cabins, each built high on precarious-looking stilts. I had my doubts about entering such structures. What if they slid down the mountain? Kieran, who I hoped knew more than me, seemed immune to such doubts. He led us, horses and all, up the stairs to the door of the first cabin. Banging on it, he shouted a greeting over the noise of the storm. A long moment later, a man with a face like the craggy mountain opened the door, frowning as he took in our bedraggled, soaked forms.

"Please, sir," Kieran said, "we need shelter."

The man observed us for a silent moment until I was sure he would turn us away, despite the squall.

"We have coin." Kieran jiggled the purse tied to his waist.

Kieran's quiet offer roused the man. He shook his head gruffly. "No need for that. Well met in Shaddai's peace."

He opened the door. Kieran led Paddy inside while I took the horses around the back to the stable. The stable was mostly empty, except for a couple of pigs, so I didn't feel bad about our mounts taking up the dry straw. Removing our packs, I shook as much water as I could from them, then hurriedly wiped the horses down before heading inside.

All heads turned when I entered the small, plain cabin. A large table with benches took up the center of the room. Kieran sat at the table with a steaming mug in his hands. A middle-aged, thick-waisted woman stood in front of the fire rubbing an unhappy Paddy down with a blanket. Two young girls sat near the kitchen, huddled together and whispering. One of them, a blonde about thirteen years old, couldn't take her eyes off Kieran.

The man pointed to a place beside Kieran. "Sit. My name is Rol Amait. This is my wife, Enda, and my daughters, Allia and Shanna."

I obliged him and accepted a cup of tea. The storm continued raging outside. I gave a silent prayer of thanks for the respite from it.

Enda dragged Paddy behind a curtain and, after a short exchange, which she dominated, he came out wearing nothing but a blanket and an embarrassed expression. I preferred to stay in my wet clothes.

"Where are you from?" Rol asked, blunt.

Eager to protect Kieran's identity, I answered. "Kieran is from Citadel, and I am from Lor."

"Lor?" Rol asked. "You don't have their coloring." I felt a flush rise up my neck. Shaddai, how I hated to admit my bastardy!

Kieran interceded. "Lance is different." And he left it at that.

"And the boy?"

"We met him on the trail. He won't say where he's from," I volunteered. We all turned to stare at Paddy, who felt no compunction to inform us.

Enda interrupted us with bowls of hot gruel. Everyone gathered around the table, even the girls, who continued giggling amongst themselves. Kieran made polite conversation, ever the diplomat. I looked around the small cabin, noticing how everything was fashioned from rough logs, down to the two leisure chairs sitting across from each other in front of the fireplace. Pelts covered the walls and lay stacked in one corner. The family wore simple woolen clothing and used utensils and tools hewn by their own hands.

Merchants, perhaps, didn't frequent this area of the Land.

Night fell soon after dinner, and Rol announced that his family would retire. Enda supplied us with extra blankets before disappearing up the ladder to the loft with the rest of her family. Kieran and I stood leaning on the mantle, letting the fire finish drying our clothes, while Paddy remained at the table, braiding several pieces of leather together for a belt.

The rain still beat on, a steady drumroll. "Strange storm," Kieran commented. "Very powerful."

Something about his tone made me cast a sidelong glance at him. "I didn't cause it," I whispered furiously.

He crooked a grin at me. "I didn't suggest that you did."

"Humph," I replied.

We looked into the flames. Kieran said, "Much has happened since we met. I feel, somehow, that we have much work to do together, and that this trip will take us longer and farther than we anticipate."

My stomach churned. "You're worrying again."

He cocked his head at me. *Are you so sure?* He spoke the words in my mind.

I straightened with a jerk, my heart convulsing. He looked at me steadily. *Can you answer?* he asked. I heard—felt—his surprise at the ease of this strange communication.

I shook my head, trying to contain the fear choking my throat. Kieran wouldn't hurt me purposefully. I doubted he could even hurt me *accidentally*. Still, this bizarre mind-talk frightened me. Answering him—assuming that were even possible—

would change me in some deep and inexplicable way that I couldn't articulate. Nor did I want to.

"What is going on?" Paddy asked with uncanny perception.

I regarded him, wondering if I looked as spooked as I felt. "Nothing."

He gave me an unbelieving expression, but then announced, "I'm going to sleep. I don't feel well."

With that, he crawled onto a pallet within range of the fire and fell asleep almost immediately.

Kieran still looked at me. "You hate it," he said aloud.

I didn't try to deny it. "It's unnatural. Freakish. Where did it come from? Why us?"

"Who knows? We are different from other people, Lance. Revel in it. Don't fear it."

"Perhaps you are the only different one," I said, my voice a whisper. "Perhaps you can speak thus to everybody."

"No. I didn't let on, but I've tried with Paddy. There's no one else to try it with. It doesn't matter, though. I know that somehow, this communication is limited only to you, and I think I might know why."

"Tell me." My heart jumped.

"Not now. It's only a guess. I'll tell you more if my suspicions are proven true."

I didn't push it. Speculation only made my head hurt.

He hadn't taken his gaze off me. His eyes seemed to burn. "I will not mind-speak you intentionally, if you wish," he offered.

A tempting offer. It would not stop the flow of truth, however. Neither would it forestall the destiny Shaddai had planned for us.

"Do as you wish," I said faintly.

He nodded, seeming to understand my reservations.

The rain slackened to a gentle, constant shower. Despite the soothing sound and the fact that we lay snug and warm inside, protected from the elements, I ached for Lor, and for old, innocent times.

The next morning when Paddy awoke, his forehead burned with fever and his breath made a thin, wheezing sound. He didn't even sneer when Kieran asked him how he felt, which worried me. Enda threw her hands up in the air, muttered about fool boys running around in terrible storms, and cooked him a broth.

The rain continued. I drifted onto the porch after breakfast and stood next to Rol. Together, we watched the drizzle.

Presently, Rol's neighbors lined their own porch, staring at me in shameless curiosity. Rol raised his hand and spoke a greeting, but he didn't elaborate on my arrival.

"How often do you have such storms?" I asked.

"Not often. Once every few years. This year, we've had two." He glanced at me out of the corner of his eye. Dear Shaddai, *he* wasn't implying that we had something to do with this storm . . . was he?

"You three were headed through the pass?" he asked.

I nodded and told him of the earthquake that had closed Cantwin Pass. He didn't seem surprised.

"The earthquake hit hard here as well. Three of my neighbors had damaged cabins."

I peered through the rain to the other cabins, but I couldn't discern anything.

"What business brings you here?" Rol asked with a rude edge.

We had dropped the university story when we had passed the last turnoff to the university towns, so I told him that Kieran was a nobleman seeking confirmation of his heritage, and I was his guardsman. Rol's stony expression did not alter. After a moment, he commented, "We are Shaddai's people here. We follow Shaddai's laws. We will house you until the young one recovers, but you must labor for your keep when the rain stops."

I agreed, relieved. Paddy could recover in peace, and nothing else mattered.

We spent the rest of the day in relative quiet. Kieran busied himself sewing together a blanket from the hides of the animals we had eaten so far. Rol's daughter, Allia, sat next to him and flirted outrageously. I wandered about, restless and useless. When I saw Rol's other daughter heading my way with a big smile on her face, I retreated to where Paddy lay. He slept fitfully, whimpering now and again. I watched him, wishing I could do something to help.

Enda came up behind me and put her hands on her wide hips. She looked down at me, unsmiling. "If he weren't so thin, he wouldn't have gotten sick."

I didn't say anything in my defense, and she gave me a dirty look and went off to drag her daughter away from Kieran.

Kieran, thus freed, joined me. He hunkered down by Paddy's pallet. Paddy's whimpers turned to mumbles.

"Mother! Father!" and other words, garbled. I wondered yet again about his past.

Kieran laid a hand on Paddy's brow. The boy calmed, and Kieran gave him an affectionate smile.

Some time later, two of Rol's neighbors banged on the door. They visited for an hour, on the pretense of updating Rol on the storm's effects on other members of the community. They gaped at us nearly the entire time. At one point, I smiled and waved at them, but that caused them to look away in embarrassment. They left soon after, without ever saying a word to us. Strange people.

Paddy got worse. Kieran and I spent a long night taking turns sitting up with him, keeping him cool by sponging his forehead and chest and beating on his back when he became too congested to breathe properly. Enda smeared a foul-smelling ointment all over his chest and back that relieved his congestion. She got up to check on him several times in the night, which worried me.

The next morning ushered in a Worship Day, and everyone left to congregate at a nearby house for services. No one invited us. Paddy slept quieter that morning. The long night had sapped him of color and flesh, and—thankfully—the fever. I no longer feared that we might lose him.

The rain stopped, allowing the sun to break through the clouds. The forest glistened from the remaining moisture and the air smelled sweet and clean. I hiked down to look at the pass and the river, which flowed in rushing brown torrents. Even if

Paddy had been perfectly healthy, we couldn't travel that way for a while.

Several hours later, Rol's family returned home with two neighbors, a man and his wife. Enda and the girls worked in the kitchen to produce a simple but filling meal of bread and stewed meat. The couple spoke to Kieran and me, but I sensed that they didn't trust us. When Shanna grabbed two pails and headed for the well, I offered to carry them for her and she accepted.

We went carefully, helping one other across the soggy ground. At the well, I tied the rope around the handle of one of the buckets and lowered it into the water. As I cranked it upward, I asked, "Do you like me?"

She looked up at me through long eyelashes. "Yes, very much."

I tried to combat the warm flush inching up my neck. "Your people . . . they don't seem to."

"Oh, that," she said, unconcerned. "They are wary because of the dark priests that passed by here several months ago."

"Dark priests?" I asked in alarm.

"Four of them came through and stole the weaver's little girl. The men tracked them down and there was a terrible battle. The priests are buried out there somewhere." She gestured to the northeast. "The elders have been more cautious since."

We returned to the cabin, spilling at least half the water on the treacherous journey. Rol frowned when he saw me accompanying his daughter, but he didn't say anything.

&

As it happened, we stayed with Rol's family in the community called Gavin's Stead for nearly two weeks. At first, Paddy lay weak and ghost-like on his pallet, refusing nourishment and sleeping often. It took almost a full week before he snarled at me. The more he regained his strength, the more confinement wore on his nerves. Kieran often read to him from a thin book of verse. I liked to sit and listen as well. I didn't understand most of what Kieran read, and I know Paddy didn't either, but the words were so rare and the stories so different that we both listened eagerly.

The day after that first Worship Day, Kieran and I began laboring for our keep. We hunted with the other men, stalking animals and cleaning our kills. We fished in the overflowing streams, carried water for the women, and helped repair homes and barns damaged by the storm. Gavin's Stead, named so after the man who had settled here some years ago, consisted of two dozen adults and a like number of children. The people were taciturn, practical and on edge.

Allia, for her part, accepted us freely, undoubtedly because of her incurable fascination with Kieran. She contrived to be near him at all times until Rol got wind of her foolishness and ordered her to stop it. She obeyed only when he watched her.

"Your nobles may not have to find you a wife after all," I told him one evening, smiling. "You may have found one yourself."

Kieran looked at me blankly. I motioned to Allia, whose gentle eyes lit on him from across the room. She turned away, embarrassed, when she saw us looking at her.

"I'm afraid that she and I could never be," he said with a pained look about his eyes. "I must marry a woman of the same class. And, to save trouble in the future, I might as well marry one with her heritage lines all laid out."

"Always practical, aren't you?"

Paddy, the devil, had not been privy to our conversation, so he teased Kieran about Allia's behavior whenever possible. Kieran bore the taunts patiently, saying nothing to Paddy. When Paddy and I were alone, I threatened to tie a rope to his wrists and make him run along behind my horse when we departed this village. Paddy stopped badgering Kieran after that.

On our twelfth day in Gavin's Stead, when Paddy could walk about for short periods, Kieran and I rose early for an excursion into the forest to chop wood. Rol and three other villagers accompanied us. We hiked into the misty morning for at least half an hour before finding an adequate field. Kieran, Rol, and a man named Cal went to the north side of the field to work. The other two men, brothers named Mikel and Donne, and I chose a fine, tall oak within sight of Kieran and the others.

Mikel and I worked as a team. He did one stroke, and I the next. Slowly, we made headway into the rock-hard wood. Within a few strokes, my arms began aching and sweat soaked my face and chest. At last, the tree cracked and we stepped back as it crashed to the ground with a great boom. Donne set to work dividing it into smaller pieces. After a brief rest and a swig of water from my companion's water skin, we moved on to another tree. Shaddai, but this would be a *long* day.

We had no more started swinging our axes again when a violent yank catapulted me from my body into a different world. After a spinning moment of disorientation, I realized that I hadn't been separated from my body, but my body had changed. I padded along silently, low to the ground, my muscles and sinews gliding me across the forest floor with flawless, fluid precision.

The tops of the trees spanned an unimaginable distance above me. The bushes around me seemed very tall. My belly rumbled. I wanted meat, and death, and the sweet, warm taste of blood on my tongue, sliding down my throat. Suddenly, I realized what had happened. A mountain cat, sleek and powerful, had been driven down from the high mountaintop by the earthquake and the storm. And I was that cat.

Muted yellow colors surrounded me. Sharp smells and clear sounds guided me forward. A loud, steady, puzzling noise pounded my sensitive ears. The instigators of the awful sound came into view. Three fleshy creatures, weak and soft. Food, at last. My eyes fell on the nearest one, the dark-haired one. Padded feet sprinted forward—

"Kieran!" I screamed, thrust at once back into my own body. Vivid color flared all around me as my hearing and sense of smell dulled. I threw aside the axe and charged toward Kieran.

An open field separated me from him. I ran, ridiculously weak and slow on just two legs. The cat bounded ahead, terrible, too fast. Rol cried out, and Kieran snapped his head toward the beast. The cat leaped, muscles rippling under smooth tan fur, long white teeth exposed to the open air. Kieran threw out a hand to shield himself.

144

I would not reach him in time. But I would *not* let him be hurt. I threw all my energy, all my willpower, into one thought. "No!" It came out as a scream as well. My hand jerked outward, just like Kieran's.

The cat struck Kieran, but I bled. Searing pain, bright red blood. I ran on. Kieran fell backward. The cat swiped a powerful, maiming claw across his chest. I stumbled and glanced at my chest. Savage cuts, welling with blood. Kieran's companions rushed the cat, yelling and swinging their axes. Startled and outnumbered, the cat bounded back into the forest, coat bloody and belly unfilled.

I slowed and stopped. Blood soaked my chest. My companions raced up behind me, exclaiming. I barely heard them. Kieran got to his feet, staring at his hand and chest in obvious incomprehension. Then he looked up and saw me, and something frightening passed between us. In that instant, I became aware of the inevitability of our destinies, linked, our minds and souls twined by the love of Shaddai into a rope that could not be broken. I had never felt anything so immense and awesome. So terrible.

Kieran rushed toward me, his face twisted with concern.

His face was very pale. "It isn't possible," he murmured, reaching out to touch the blood on my shredded tunic. "You've–you've—"

"Taken the blow for him," Rol finished in a stern, loud voice. Alarm rang in sharp tones through my senses.

"It is as we feared, my brothers," Rol proclaimed. "They are despisers of Shaddai, priests of the dark."

Chapter Twelve

"Seize them!" Rol thundered, and the others grabbed us. Shocked, I didn't put up the slightest resistance. "We cannot let creatures such as these survive! Come, my brothers, let us take them to the village to be destroyed."

Kieran jerked away, his face flushed. "You'll kill us? Just like that?"

"We've dealt with Shaddai-forsaken demons like you before." Rol's hard voice shook with loathing. "Our only defense is to strike before you have the chance to work your foul magic on us and our young."

If I'd had any doubt about Rol's intentions before, his words dispelled it. A sudden urgency gripped me.

146

"Kieran, run!" I might be able to fend them off long enough for him to escape.

A canvas of emotion unraveled across his face—defiance, disbelief, indignance at my request. Three of the men grabbed Kieran again, and the moment of opportunity when he might have acted passed. Kieran struggled, kicking and cursing, to no avail. I didn't bother to struggle. I felt numb, except for a dull throbbing in my chest and hand and the wet feel of dripping blood.

"They haven't tried to hurt us. Do they truly deserve death?" Cal asked, voice faltering and eyes jumping from companion to companion.

"They are evil!" Mikel snapped. "Their power comes straight from the hearts of the dark lords that live past the mountains."

Cal shut up, effectively cowed.

"What about Paddy?" I blurted out.

"He is only a boy," Rol said. "We will cleanse him from your filth."

Small solace, that.

The men dragged us to the front of Rol's cabin and threw us down beside the well. Donne ran to get rope to tie our hands with. The entire settlement appeared, gawking. Rol's daughters clutched each other, tears streaking their faces. I tried to smile encouragement at them.

Blood flowed in steady pulses from my wounds, but I didn't expect that anyone would bind them before they hacked us to pieces with their axes. The world seemed very bright and clear, each moment a slow-moving wheel. My head buzzed, and I felt the steady 'thump, thump, thump' of my heartbeat. Would I know when it stopped?

I focused on the scene as if disconnected from what was happening. Rol, accusing us of sorcery. The elders, outraged. Women, crying out as they sheltered their children behind their skirts. And that fateful word from Rol's lips, "Death!"

The men jerked our arms behind us and bound them. Two of the elders approached with axes. A heavy kind of sadness consumed me. Kieran knelt beside me, sweaty and panting. I felt his fear, a great dread, filling up a corner of my mind. He shouldn't have to die, too.

He jerked toward me, his face a fierce mask. "Don't you give up!" he hissed.

His passion jolted something inside me. "I won't," I answered, whether through my tongue or my mind, I don't know.

A great, crashing noise sounded, branches breaking and wood cracking. A horse screamed, followed by a high-pitched whoop. The crowd tumbled aside and I saw Paddy, wild-eyed and snarling. He perched high on Silvereye, Goldie's reins clutched in his hand. My horse skidded to a halt beside us. Steel flashed in Paddy's hand, and I felt my bonds fall away. We swung onto our horses, Paddy scrambling up in front of me on Silvereye.

We jolted away, the crowd following us with a great roar. Cut loose after so many days of idleness, the horses dashed across the stony ground and ran break-neck along the rushing water filling the pass. The outrage of our pursuers was like a hot brand on the back of my neck.

We rode for what seemed like hours without a break until the blood drained from my head and I sagged against Paddy, quite helpless. He pushed me

148

back, but I fell again. Then he turned around, his eyes widening at the sight of my blood leaking everywhere, bright and spreading.

"Kieran!" Paddy shouted.

Suddenly, Kieran appeared at my side, taking in the front of my tunic with a sharp gaze. "Hang on, Lance!" he ordered.

How silly. Of course I would hang on. Falling off the horse would be most dangerous. Painful, too. I grinned to myself. Kieran pulled me off Silvereye's back. My knees buckled as soon as I hit the ground. Kieran helped me lie down. He yanked off his shirt and tossed it at Paddy. "Rip this up into strips and bring me the water bags!"

Kieran pulled at my ruined shirt. Using Paddy's little knife, which had somehow appeared, he gently cut my shirt. I felt nothing until he came to the part where my blood had dried and stuck to the cloth. Biting my lip, I remained silent.

Kieran had obviously never bound anyone's wounds before. His shaking hands made him clumsy, and in the end, he tied the bandages too tightly. When he finished, he pulled me to my feet and sat me on Goldie's back with much huffing and puffing, my tattered tunic barely hanging on my back. He climbed up behind me. I didn't know why. I didn't feel *that* bad.

"My gear!" I exclaimed. The red flag of my ancestry had been with my pack at Rol's home.

"Relax," Kieran said in my ear. "Paddy brought everything."

The little ragamuffin sat up taller at the mention of his name.

"How did you save us?" I asked. How strange and distant my voice sounded.

"I've been feeling better. I even go out sometimes. I followed you this morning when you and Kieran went to cut wood. I saw everything." He looked meaningfully at me. What could I say? I didn't know what had happened any more than he did.

"When I realized what they meant to do, I ran back to the barn and readied everything," he explained. "No one even thought to look for me."

"You saved our lives. Thank you," I said in all sincerity.

Paddy flushed in pleasure.

"We should not speak. Sound carries far out here," Kieran said.

He was right. We spoke no more for the rest of the afternoon and traveled at a moderate pace. Mindful of the horses, Kieran steered us away from the rocky banks whenever he could. At twilight, we stopped at a boulder-lined alcove, which sheltered our fire from view. Kieran half-carried me to a fallen log, where I rested, propping my elbows on my knees to support my head. My head alternately whirled and pounded. Nausea twisted my stomach, and my mouth felt dry.

I felt guilty for not helping Kieran and Paddy unpack the horses and ready the camp for the night, but when I attempted to rise, Kieran jabbed a finger at me and snapped, "Sit!"

Like a naughty hound, I sat.

Presently, Paddy sat next to me and pulled out several wheat cakes pilfered from Enda's kitchen. He offered me one, but I declined. Food held no appeal for me. Kieran came over, bearing an armful of tinder and several good-sized logs. He threw them into the fire with increasing force. The cords on his neck stood out, as did the veins on his tight fists. He ignored me, bending to arrange the firewood.

"What's wrong?" I asked.

Paddy observed without comment. The small tower of kindling beneath Kieran's fingers collapsed, and he swiped at the tinder in frustration. Then he stomped off twenty paces or so and leaned with one hand against a tree, his back toward us. I looked at Paddy, who shrugged. After a moment of uneasy silence, I stood, pausing while the vertigo passed. I teetered over to Kieran, whose shoulders stiffened as I neared.

"Why are you angry? Is it the colonists?"

He looked at me with burning eyes. "No. It is you."

Startled, I blurted out, "Me?"

"How dare you take my wounds from me? I'm not a puling infant. Do not treat me as if I need your constant protection!"

I did not bother to tell him that I hadn't intended on taking the cat's paws for him. Instead, I yelped, "But you *do* need my constant protection. I am your guardsman!"

He seized the front of my shirt, causing me to stumble into the bole of the tree. "I want to fight my own battles, Lance. I want to take my own scrapes! Can't you see that?"

I shook free of his grip, confused and defensive. "No, I can't. I won't stand by and watch you be injured when I can do something about it. But for Shaddai's sake, Kieran, be fair. I didn't even know I *could* take your wounds as mine before today."

He fixed his eyes on some distant point, his jaw hard. "You must pledge upon your honor to never do anything like that again."

"No!" I shouted, getting angry myself. "As your guardsman, I vowed to give up my life for yours."

"Damn your vows!" he declared. "I hereby release you from them!"

His words stopped me cold. I took a long, deep breath before calmly replying, "I vowed to be your guardsman under Shaddai. You can order me from your side, and despise me, and curse me for the rest of your days, but it will change nothing. I will not break my vow."

He stared away from me in impotent anguish, then ground out in a shaking voice, "Leave me alone."

Gladly, I obliged him, walking back to the log and sitting down, suddenly even more drained than before our confrontation. Paddy had started the fire and pretended that he hadn't heard Kieran and me fighting. My body ached, and I longed to lie down. But that would require getting up to retrieve my blankets. Besides, how could I sleep with this awful knot of tension in my stomach? After a while, Kieran came over to the fire, hunkering down across from me. His face was hard as granite.

I hung my head in misery. Slowly, I became aware of the night sounds—the buzzing of fireflies, the wind through the pines. Life had been so simple when I was that mountain cat. Predator, prey, mate, rest. No worrying about vows and strange powers, lurking evil and untouchable good.

Sometime later, I felt an arm around my shoulders. Jerking awake fully, I saw Kieran supporting me, his anger gone.

"Come, you are exhausted. I have laid out your bed."

Paddy lay sleeping not far from my own empty, inviting blankets. I shook my head. "I won't sleep while you're angry with me."

It had been a rule in our household, growing up. At the time, it had seemed stupid and cumbersome, especially when I had to apologize for some imagined slight to my brothers and sisters, but now I could see the wisdom in it.

Kieran sighed and regarded me through dark-ringed eyes. "I am not angry with you any longer. If our roles were reversed, I would probably do the same for you. But please, from now on, use discretion. I don't want you harmed on my account. You are my truest friend, and I love you like a brother."

A lump accumulated in my throat as I sat there staring at him helplessly, trying to think of a worthy reply. But Kieran waved off my stumbling attempts and helped me to bed. Sleep claimed me within three breaths.

Morning. A cool breeze, slanted sunlight, and the sounds of my companions' movements. Then, a warm hand on my shoulder and a quiet voice in my ear. "Lance, wake."

"No . . ." I moaned. "Let me die in peace."

"Come on, Lance," Kieran said with a patient sigh. "We must put as much distance as possible between us and the settlers. Here, drink this." He handed me a cup.

I took a sip and wrinkled my nose. "Water!" I had expected strong wine or even hot tea.

"If you can complain, you can ride. Get up," Kieran said.

I scowled but held out my hand, and he helped me upright. I hobbled around, groaning and moaning like an old man, until my muscles loosened enough for Kieran and Paddy to help me climb onto Silvereye's back.

I only began to feel vaguely human again after several hours of riding, when I grew hungry. We stopped by a stream to rest the horses, where Paddy picked me a handful of berries and fed me one of the cakes from the previous night. I felt better until I noticed the sky darkening above us.

"By all the Powers of the Land! It's not going to rain again!"

Paddy and Kieran exchanged a look. "Perhaps not," Kieran commented. "The One may yet take pity on you. Or on us."

"What do you mean by that?"

"I mean that you are as sour as old milk today, my friend," he said, laughing. I hadn't heard him laugh for a long time, and I liked the sound of it. But I wasn't about to let *him* know that.

"Well, you had your chance at ill humor. Now I'm having mine."

I stumbled over to Silvereye again, in the hopes that I could mount without help. No such luck. Kieran came over, unasked, and pushed me up until I managed to hook a leg over my horse's back.

As we rode, the scenery distracted me from my physical complaints—beautiful, tangled wilderness, unspoiled and carpeted with strawberries and raspberries, plums and persimmons bright with color. For a while, Paddy and I counted the number of standing trees blackened and riven from lightning strikes, keeping a separate tally of the older trees, fallen already and in various stages of decay.

By early afternoon, though, even the thriving Land could not keep me from noticing the way my back ached. My bandages rubbed against my wounds, making them hot and itchy. When we met up with a stream, I dismounted and stripped off my clothes, letting the cool water wash away the grime and dried blood.

"Lance!" Kieran cried. "You're hurt! Get out of there!"

"You yourself heard Paddy. Water is scarce on the plains. Now is the last opportunity we might have for a good bath."

"You're getting your bandages wet!"

Well, so I was. I ripped them off.

Kieran called me names, but I ignored him, intent on picking at my chest and hand. They were already scabbing over, healing much faster than I had expected. The fresh mountain air must have been good for me.

When it became apparent that I wasn't coming out of the water, Kieran and Paddy joined me. We splashed each other, skipped rocks, and caught flies before lying out on the flat rocks surrounding the water, sunning ourselves like lizards. I was drowsing, enjoying the heat, when a far-off sound caught my attention. It seemed to come from somewhere within the stand of scrub brush and young poplars nearby, a sound like high-pitched squawking.

No, make that honking. I sat up on my elbows, and when the wounds on my chest stretched, I wished I hadn't. Honking wasn't the right word, either. *Squealing*—that was it! The squealing was joined by the cries of a frustrated human. And the sounds were getting louder.

I moved toward my weapons on shore. Silently, Paddy and Kieran did the same. Kieran sent me a worried look—the settlers? But it seemed unlikely that the squealing, which reminded me of a herd of angry pigs, could have anything to do with them. A moment later, the underbrush began rustling as though a pack of wild dogs were thrashing around in it. A man's half-hysterical curses punctuated the squealing.

The brush parted, and a rickety pushcart full of six angry, pink piglets came jerking out, propelled by a red-faced, curly-haired young man. He wore a filthy peasant's tunic and a tiny brimless hat perched askew on a rather large head.

"People!" he bleated. "Thank Shaddai!" Relief flooded his features. He stumbled toward us.

"Halt!" I barked, threatening him with my sword. "Who are you?"

He stopped, eyes bulging. "Is this the road through the Cantwins? I've been looking for it for days! Uncle Mic said it would only take four days to get there, but I've already been traveling for seven days, so when I saw the trail, I took it. Then it got smaller and smaller and finally, it disappeared, but I kept following the direction because I knew it had to lead somewhere. Trails shouldn't just appear in the middle of nowhere and then stop, should they? Well, they do, because this one just stopped. That's why I was pushing through the bushes. Elwin."

"What are you blathering about?" I demanded.

He blinked. His protruding brown eyes reminded me of my mother's favorite milk cow. "You asked my name," he clarified. "It's Elwin."

Elwin began unloading the piglets from the pushcart. Their squeals of indignation turned into grunts of happiness as they wiggled about in fresh green grass.

"I think you can put your sword down now, Lance," Kieran commented, looking amused. "He seems harmless enough."

Reluctantly, I did so. Elwin loped up to us, a grin splitting open his face and revealing crooked teeth. "Well met in Shaddai's peace."

We introduced ourselves, and Paddy asked, "What are you doing with all these pigs?"

"Taking them to market at Downwind." He scratched his head and looked around. "At least, I hope I am. This is the road through the Cantwins, isn't it?"

"Yes," Kieran admitted. "But I can't recommend that you take this route."

"Why not?"

"Because the settlers at the mouth of the pass are likely to mistake you for a dark priest and lop your head off. Which is what they tried to do to us," I said.

He gaped. "A dark priest?"

"They are running about the Land, apparently. You have not encountered any?"

He gave me a blank stare and shook his head. "I have never left home before, though."

"Come join us, then," Kieran offered. "And tell us about yourself."

His plain face lit up, and he rushed over like an excited child. He pointed out his family's isolated homestead on my map and then rambled off into a lengthy explanation of the physical characteristics, likes, dislikes, and various personality quirks of every member of said obscenely huge family. Less than halfway through, Paddy wandered away to play with the piglets, who seemed to like the company of humans. I set up camp and fried a hank of ham and some corn cakes Paddy had lifted off the settlers.

Elwin stopped talking and sniffed the air. Kieran took the hint.

"Please," he said. "Eat with us. We have plenty to share."

"Thank you!" Elwin dashed back to his pushcart to dig through his possessions for a wooden bowl, which he handed to me with a voracious gleam in his eye.

The bowl was encrusted with something brown. Rather disgusted, I looked at Elwin for an explanation. "It's porridge. I've had only porridge and carrots to eat since I left home."

No wonder he was so eager for a meal. I banged the bowl on a nearby rock to dislodge some of the dried food, then served him. Elwin set to eating like a toothless mule in a fresh patch of clover, complete with smacking lips, chomping noises, and appreciative burps. Loose food particles fell from his mouth regularly, but he deftly caught them in his bowl, apparently skilled from long practice.

I looked at Kieran, who shrugged, and forced myself to eat, although now, my appetite had

diminished substantially. Afterward, we sat around the
fire, relaxing. Elwin realized that he hadn't finished
telling Kieran about his family, so he started
yammering on about them again. Still weakened by
my wound, I lay down on my pallet to rest for a
moment and promptly fell into a deep, exhausted
sleep.

I dreamed that wild animals were attacking a
screeching child. Frightened by the image, I awoke
and looked at the night around me. The brightness of
the high mountain stars revealed Elwin sleeping
nearby, a silver line of drool dripping from the corner
of his lip. The source of my nightmare became
clear—his snores. I had never heard anything
remotely like the whistling, shrieking, and teeth-
crunching that emanated from his mouth. The piglets
didn't seem to mind the noises, though. They slept
huddled together, in a big, pink mass, by his feet. He
had looped a frayed rope around their necks to keep
them together.

Although I dearly wanted to kick him, I restrained
myself and instead nudged him with my foot until he
turned onto his side. Then he started snoring even
louder, something that I didn't think was humanly
possible. After a while, I gave up the idea of getting
any more sleep that night.

At sunrise, when Kieran awoke, I already had half
the camp packed up. After some initial face rubbing
and a trip to empty his bladder, Kieran set about
cutting the remaining chunk of ham for breakfast.
Wordlessly, he extended my portion to me. We
watched Paddy and Elwin, who were crouched down
on the opposite side of the water. Elwin was pointing
at the plants alongside the pond and explaining

something to Paddy. The piglets wandered around both of them.

"Tell me you didn't invite him to travel with us," I said.

Kieran looked surprised. "No, not yet. But we'll be traveling the same direction for at least a few days. You don't want him along?"

"By all means, invite him. But don't expect him to live out the week."

Kieran guffawed. In a moment, he sobered. "You're serious."

"Entirely."

At that moment, Paddy looked up and saw that I was awake. Motioning for Elwin to follow him, he jumped up and ran toward me. "Lance! Elwin knows all about plants. He showed me how to use them to cure wounds, and lower a fever, and lots of other things. He is going to teach them to me as long as he stays with us. Can he stay with us, Lance? It's only for a couple of days. Please?"

I swallowed. "Uh ...." I looked to Kieran, hoping for support. Conveniently, he was studying the dirt as his feet. Great. I fumbled for words before inspiration struck. "Paddy, perhaps Elwin doesn't want to stay. Have you even asked him?"

"Not exactly . . ."

"Oh, I don't mind," Elwin enthused. "We can travel together until the Downwind crossroads. I welcome the company."

Yes, but I don't, I wanted to say. I managed to restrain myself.

Paddy grabbed my hands and implored, "Please, Lance. Pleeeeeeeeeeeeeease!"

"But—"

"Lance!"

Elwin stayed.

The following day, we breached the summit of the pass after a strenuous three-hour climb. Kieran kept pestering me to go slow and take it easy. Finally, I stopped in my tracks and plucked my shirt off to show him that my wounds hadn't torn open. Elwin, who had managed to maintain a running dialogue about the types of plant leaves that made good tasting tea while steering the pushcart around boulders and over uneven spots in the trail, dropped the arms of the pushcart with a thud and rushed over to examine my wounds. Clucking in dismay, he dug around in his satchel and pulled out a pinch of brown powder that he sprinkled on my healing skin. It burned as though a nest of hornets had stung me.

"Ow! What on earth did you put on me?"

"That means it's working," Elwin said happily.

"Like hell it is!" I yelped and dumped half a water skin over my chest to wash the powder away.

Unfazed by my agony, Elwin picked up the pushcart and trotted off ahead of us. I followed, thinking evil thoughts until the beauty of the surroundings distracted me. Up here, the sun seemed to burn hotter and the pine trees stood silent watch over the still, bony hump of the mountains. Cascading hills spread out below us and dissolved into a smeared blue horizon.

Paddy gestured toward that horizon. "We will reach the plains tomorrow. We should be on watch. Here, the Bel-Midron roam."

That night, we camped on the lee of a hill. I made sure I went to bed before Elwin, but his snores woke me again in the night.

I shook him awake. "You're snoring!"

"Huh?" He blinked, owl-eyed. "Sorry."

He wandered off, his blanket trailing on the ground behind him, and found a bed near a boulder some fifty paces away. His snores were faint enough that I dozed off again.

In the morning, Paddy crouched near the fire, stirring a pot with a stick. Kieran, up already as usual, sat opposite me, sipping a steaming cup.

"Paddy made us tea," he said, expressionless.

"Yes!" Paddy crowed, dipping a cup in the pot and handing it to me. "Have some."

He dashed off to awaken Elwin, who came stumbling up to the camp fire, his shaggy brown hair sticking up at all angles. Paddy shoved a cup of tea in his face, too, and watched eagerly as each of us sipped the bitter brown mess. Somehow, I refrained from making gagging noises, though it wasn't easy.

Elwin took a taste and then asked, "What did you put in here?"

"It's mint, chamomile, and a secret ingredient. See if you can guess what it is."

Somehow, each of us managed to choke down his whole cup. Paddy stared intently at us the entire time, leaving no opportunity to toss the liquid into the fire when he wasn't looking. He poked at the dirt with a stick. Apparently, he'd used it to stir the tea, if the remnants in my cup were any indication.

"Something wrong, boy?" I asked. My head felt thick of a sudden.

"No!" Paddy yelped. "Why would you think that?" He jumped to his feet. "I'll break camp." He scurried around, gathering our supplies while the three of us watched, listless.

A thump sounded. I looked over to see Elwin, curled up on the ground beside the rock he had been sitting on, fast asleep. Now, that was odd.

Kieran put his hand to his head. "I don't feel so good." His words sounded slurred.

I tried to comment, but my tongue felt as big as a summer sausage.

Kieran groaned and yawned. "Tired." He leaned back against a fallen log.

Paddy had stopped packing and looked at me with the strangest expression. I tried to get up and go to him, but my body would not obey me. I made it to my knees, and reached out for him. But then my hand sank down slowly, unaccountably heavy. The rest of me followed momentarily.

I awoke some time later, my mouth gaping open and my throat dry. Dizzy and groggy, I sat up. Kieran lay sprawled out across from me, snoring softly. Elwin was standing at the edge of camp, looking lost and dazed. Something seemed strange about the campsite. After a long moment of dull staring, I realized that Paddy, Goldie, and half our supplies were missing.

"Paddy!" I croaked like a frog.

Kieran slept through my cursing and flailing, so I slapped his face lightly.

"Wake up!"

He tried half-heartedly to push me away before peeling back a tired eyelid to see my disgruntled face.

"Paddy stole your horse," I informed him.

He sat up too quickly and vomited. Away from me, luckily. I gave him plenty of room until he was through. He sat holding his head in his hands. "Are you sure?"

"Believe me, I'm sure. The demon spawn must have drugged our tea …" I trailed off as Elwin sat heavily across from us, then gritted out, "How do you suppose Paddy learned to identify a plant that could be used to knock us unconscious?"

Elwin flushed. "He seemed so eager to learn. How was I to know that he would use the knowledge against us?"

I thought through the haze in my brain, then turned to Kieran. "Why would he steal from us now, after all we've been through together?"

Kieran shrugged. "Who knows? Maybe he has somewhere to go and he only used us to get this far."

"I can track him."

By now, he would be hours away, though. Double the weight on Silvereye would slow us down, not that it would matter much. Tracking would be slow and laborious either way.

Kieran thought. "No. We'll go on to Kesh."

I narrowed my gaze and nodded at Elwin. Kieran got up, and we walked just out of earshot.

"Tracking may not take that much time. Goldie's your favorite," I said.

"Yes, but she's a horse. You're my friend. When we find my heritage records, I'll sleep better knowing that your life is no longer in danger. Provided we keep away from mountain cats."

I didn't laugh.

We surveyed our supplies. Paddy had taken our remaining food, a water bag, a blanket, my crossbow, all the bolts I had so carefully constructed, and my hunting knife. Angered anew at the extent of his thievery, I kicked the remaining camp gear, bushes, trees, and anything else in range until Kieran offered, "He does need some protection from the dangers of the trail. He's alone now."

I sobered. Kieran was right. We had enough to manage, and we were together. Although I would never have admitted it to Paddy, I worried for his welfare.

We came to the Downwind crossroads the next afternoon. Elwin took the southerly road and disappeared around a bend, his pushcart creaking and the piglets bouncing along merrily.

"Thank Shaddai in heaven!" I proclaimed. "I have half a mind to extract a sacred promise from you that there will be no more traveling companions for us along the way."

Kieran pursed his lips as though in thought. "Would that make you happy?"

"A night without listening to Elwin snore will restore my good temper, I am certain."

He laughed. And indeed, it was so.

The day after, at mid-morning, we came to a knoll overlooking the plains. Miles and miles of yellow grass stretched out before us, broken by occasional small uplifts in the soil. There were no trees, shrubs, mountains, nothing. It was ugly, but something in the openness of the sky reminded me of my home in the Golden Hills. Kieran and I exchanged unenthusiastic shrugs and headed down the slope.

In an effort to save Silvereye's back, we took turns riding him through the yellow grass. The grass, as tall as a man's head and nearly as thick, contained troublesome burrs that wormed into breeches and boots and tunics. Insects nipped our exposed skin, swarmed in front of our eyes, and buzzed around our ears. Sweat streamed down my face and under my arms, and the scab on my hand itched like a devil. The only good thing about the place was the abundance of game hiding in the brush. In no time, we killed a fat rabbit for supper.

That evening, Kieran kicked dirt over the fire after we had roasted the rabbit. Tired from the long day and drowsy from my full stomach, it took a while for me to ask, "Why did you do that?"

"The Bel-Midron. I don't want them to know we're here."

I raised my eyebrow. While in Lor, I'd never given the Bel-Midron more than a passing thought. I had never seen one, nor did I know much about them.

Kieran cleared his throat and threaded his hands behind his head. "History was one of my favorite courses in university."

And so I learned about how at time's beginning, when all the tribes of man came together to settle into towns, the people of the Bel-Midron had joined them. But the Bel-Midron chafed in the confinement, and their restlessness propelled them onto the plains again, where they remained nomads, following the herds of deer and antelope and raiding nearby peoples. Generally, the kings of Cantwin had let the

166

plainsmen alone, and vice versa, though at times, one or the other would test their boundaries.

"The farther west one goes, the wilder the people become," Kieran explained. The moon, a silver sliver, threw milky light on his face. "They are even said to scorn the teachings of the Land and traffic with strange sorceries."

"Perhaps this is where Morrigu hails from."

"Perhaps," Kieran said absently, slowly rubbing his fingers across his jaw. "There have been rumors about that, and other things."

I hesitated, watching a falling star arc across the dark sky. My thoughts ambled down a dim path, and for once, I allowed them the journey.

"The other things . . . are you referring to the strange abilities we seem to have?"

I so hated to speak of them!

He looked me in the eye, calm and expressionless. "Yes."

"You know things you aren't saying. Things I haven't allowed you to say." I swallowed. "Have we been cursed?" My voice cracked.

Kieran smiled gently. "Blessed, rather, I should say. There are old stories of the Power, of how it comes from the Land, a holy trust laid upon our people. Father forbade talk of it. He said it was foolish old superstition."

"The bards sing about the Land," I offered tentatively. "They say it is alive like a person is alive, that its heart is the sun and its veins are the rivers. My grandfather always knew the day before a storm would gather or a horse would foal. The elders called his knowledge 'feeling the Power'."

167

"Power," Kieran repeated. Then, unexpectedly, "Your wounds, Lance. How are they?"

"Very good—nearly healed. They weren't as serious as they looked, I think."

"No, Lance. They were deep, and the blood . . . it was everywhere. But as I bound your wounds, I felt a warmth in my fingers . . ." He looked at his hands as if they weren't his. "It's hard to explain, but Power is a good word for it."

I looked down at my chest and my hand. Suddenly, the wounds there felt apart from me, as though they lived on another's skin. My stomach twisted.

"You . . . healed me?"

"I don't know," he said. His face, shadow-marked by the firelight, seemed calm and wise.

"It must be you, then, as we suspected. You are the special one, Kieran, blessed by Shaddai." It made sense. Shaddai had given him the kingdom. Why not this blessing as well? But that was not all. His goodness and gentleness, his talent for music—surely, these were indicators of his greatness.

He did not say anything for a very long moment, but only continued to stare at me as though he wanted to say something in response. Something profound and shocking. Instead, he only repeated, "I don't know."

Chapter Thirteen

The grass grew so tall here for a reason, we discovered the following day when the ground became muddy, then wet. A swamp. Kieran and I waded about in the mucky, stinking water for three torturous days before emerging, tired, reeking, and frustrated, to a pleasant, but nearly bare steppe. Our relief soon turned to nervousness as we crept along the exposed earth, afraid that every little rustle and gust of wind heralded the arrival of a band of screaming Bel-Midron raiders. Three more days of that brought us to our long-sought destination: Kesh.

We staked Silvereye and climbed a cairn of rocks about a mile from the crumbling ruins of the city.

"That can't be it," I scoffed.

"I'm afraid it is." Kieran looked as pasty-faced as I felt.

At one time, perhaps many years ago, Kesh had been a huge city full of grand homes and towering halls, cobbled roads and tall walls. Now, however, only piles of rubble, scorched and twisted, remained. Here and there, evidence of humanity protruded from amongst the debris—a half-broken column, parts of walls, small, cultivated plots and huts scavenged from the debris and pieced together haphazardly. Cook-smoke and dust filled the air. Mangy dogs sniffed the piles, and dirty children darted in and out of the warrens, their sharp, playful cries lonely amidst the desolation.

We split up and scouted the perimeter of the ruined city, keeping out of sight. The trip revealed nothing more than we'd already seen.

Kieran chewed his lip, considering our options.

"Shall we enter, then?" I prodded.

Kieran caught my arm. "We can't go charging in there. What about the Bel-Midron?"

"They seem to be absent."

"*Seeming* is different than *being*."

"I'm tired of waiting, Kieran. I want answers about strange mind powers and assassins who explode and kings who go mad. The sooner we go in there and find your birthright, the sooner we can return to Citadel and discover the truth."

Kieran's lips drew a tight line across his face. "I, too, want answers, Lance. More than you can possibly know. But we must not risk our lives foolishly."

I folded my arms and stared at him. "We can't wait until nightfall to creep in because there's no moon, and we'd have to light a torch to find our way,

170

possibly attracting even more attention than if we went in the middle of the day. But by all means, since you are the smart one, enlighten me. What shall we do instead?"

My comment inspired a glare, and he remained silent for a moment, contemplating. I could predict the trail of his thoughts. We had no place to watch the city without eventually being seen. We would definitely be spotted if we stood out here for much longer on the naked plains debating what to do.

"Come on," he said, "but let's be careful."

I smirked. "As you say, Wise One."

"Shut up, Lance."

We entered the refuse heap formerly known as Kesh with hardly a stir. The children stopped playing and regarded us curiously for a few moments before losing interest. A few rag-covered denizens cleared the path upon seeing us. I chased after several in a vain attempt to find information about the old library, but they ducked into the debris like gophers.

We wandered for quite some time down aisle after foul-smelling alleyway. Around noon, footsore and famished, I sat down on the edge of a well. Kieran joined me, and we rested in silence. I had begun recognizing landmarks—a manure heap here, a decaying deer hide there—enough to know that we had gone in a circle twice already.

A little old man wearing a ragged monk's habit scurried across the path in front of us and then froze. He backed up in surprise to take a close look at us, his brown, wrinkled face frozen in a mask of disbelief.

"Where in heaven's glory did you come from?" he squeaked.

Kieran began, "We're from—"

"No, never mind. I don't care where you're from. Just come with me. Quickly! We can't have their spies seeing you."

Kieran and I looked at each other. What choice did we have? We followed the man, who darted through a maze of rubble like a rat after a big piece of cheese, forcing us to jog to keep up with him. Finally, he guided us through a splintered old door into what passed as his dwelling place, a pile of rubble that was littered with candles and scrolls and raggedy furniture.

The man collapsed on a chair, clutching the cloth around his heart and breathing heavily. Thin and wrinkled, he was bald with a scraggly gray beard. It took him a moment to recover.

"We should be safe now."

"From the Bel-Midron?" I asked.

The man looked at me like I was an idiot. "Of course!" he cried. "How long have you been here?"

"A few hours," Kieran answered.

The man continued, "Their spies may have seen you already, then."

Kieran and I exchanged a glance, which the cleric noticed.

"Yes, my young sirs. 'Tis only Shaddai's good fortune that you missed a fearsome tribe of Bel-Midron under the leader, Searle. They left a week ago and shouldn't be back for some time. But who can tell? They are as the wind blows."

Gone. I sighed in relief. Even if their spies had seen us, they couldn't do much if their masters were absent.

"And now, young sirs, you must answer my question. Who are you?"

I answered before Kieran could. "I am Lance, from Lor, and this is my comrade, Kieran of Citadel. How may we call you, sir?"

The man straightened, pulled at his robes, and smoothed what little hair he had left. "Abelard. Speaker Abelard. By Shaddai's grace, the Bel-Midron did not cart me off into slavery when they took Kesh. They still hold the church in some awe, I suppose. Though I do my best to keep distant from them even when they are about. Life is easier that way." Abelard turned to a pot gently simmering over the small fire. A delicious odor wafted my way. "Are you hungry? I have enough to share."

Kieran shook his head and said, "No, thank—"

"That sounds wonderful!" I interrupted, sitting at a small bench in front of the table. Kieran let his irritation slip through our mental link. He was worried that we might gobble up whatever meager fare the man had to offer. But so many days on the trail—too much of it spent hungry—had made me desperate.

Abelard spooned out three steaming bowls of soup. I set about devouring mine with a fervor that made Kieran grimace in disgust. Abelard, who looked a bit taken aback at my enthusiasm, directed his comments to Kieran.

"If I may ask, what is your business here in Kesh?"

Kieran spoke between well-paced mouthfuls. "Lance and I are seeking heritage records for a claim I have pending back in Citadel."

Abelard's face broke into a grin and his nervous brown eyes glowed with excitement. "Oh, how splendid! I knew one day my work would pay off. Praise Shaddai!" Abelard clapped his hands together in thankfulness. "I am the keeper of the library, or what's left of it. Besides ministering to those few remaining here, I have been restoring it these many long years. I use the scrolls to teach the young, but I knew that one day, others would come seeking more. I must warn you, though, my work is not nearly done. You may not find what you seek."

Kieran jumped up from the table. "Come, Lance, let's hurry! This is what we've come so far to find."

Kieran's enthusiasm pleased me, but first things first.

"Sit down and let us finish our meal."

"Yes," Abelard agreed. "You must keep up your strength."

I grinned at Kieran with my mouth full—which was probably not a pretty sight—and he sat down again. Forthwith, he shoveled his food down his throat even faster than me. Abelard tried admirably to keep up with us, but he simply did not have the fortitude. When he finished, we waited patiently while the speaker went through a litany of prayers thanking Shaddai for everything from the morning sunlight to the evening chill. By the time he had finished, even I was practically jumping with excitement.

We set off again down the winding maze that led to Abelard's burrow. I didn't even try to remember the way, but I offered a prayer of my own—that Abelard would remain healthy enough to serve as our guide for as long as we might need him.

We passed several dwellings occupied by the remaining peasants, and Abelard took time to greet them and kiss their children. The children gazed at us with unabashed curiosity, but their parents refused to look us in the eye. What seemed like an hour later, after more winding passages and curious onlookers, we came to a stone building nearly the size of the Castle dining hall, with huge bronze doors bowed inward as if from a great battering ram. Scorch marks blackened one of the front walls. Inside, the walls were lined with large, long shelves, most of which had been smashed, spilling scrolls in great piles beneath them. Broken sculptures lay upon some of the scrolls. Others had water damage from the ill-maintained roof, which let the sun in to form a haphazard mosaic of light on the floor. Most of the salvageable scrolls had been moved out of the path of the elements and placed in the far right-hand corner, under a remaining section of roof. A dozen rows of shelves had been neatly restored there, holding meticulously placed scrolls. Many other scrolls awaited sorting in nearby crates.

Abelard took Kieran around the room, explaining what scrolls lay in which pile while I wandered around, picking through the occasional scroll and imagining I could read it.

Eventually, I sat on the floor and watched dust motes in the dying rays of sunlight until Kieran and Abelard joined me at a nearby table, each hefting a crate overflowing with scrolls.

"Do you require my help reading through these?" Abelard asked. My guard immediately sprang up. If he helped, we would have to tell him *what* we were looking for.

Kieran looked at me, but I shook my head.

"Thank you for your kind offer, Speaker, but I'm sure you have other duties to attend to," Kieran said.

Abelard had noticed the look between us, and he did not tread where he wasn't welcome. "As you wish, young sirs. I assume that though it is nearly dark, you would like to stay until the lamps run low tonight?"

Kieran nodded eagerly, smiling. Abelard returned his smile fondly. "I will come for you later, then." He exited in a swish of robes.

In the silence, I spoke. "I wish I could assist you, Kieran."

"You've helped enough already," he said without looking up.

I didn't know what he meant by that remark, but I didn't press the matter. I busied myself with mending my tunic, a task I seemed to do every other day or so. When the light failed me, I leaned back on a dusty old cushion and watched Kieran thumb through the scrolls before falling asleep.

A hand on my arm woke me sometime later. I looked up into Kieran's bloodshot eyes. Night lay cool and still all around us, and Abelard stood in the doorway with a sputtering torch, waiting.

"Did you find anything?" I asked.

Kieran shook his head and pointed at the crate of scrolls, barely diminished. "Don't worry—there is much more to sift through. I am confident that what we're looking for is here."

We made our way back to Abelard's hut. On the way, Kieran and I got into a whispered argument about Silvereye. Kieran didn't want me to try to find him in the dark, but I insisted. We depended on our horse. I wouldn't risk anything happening to him.

After listening to a string of directions from Abelard, I set off in the dark. A harrowing half hour later, I had stumbled through the steppe land to where my patient mount waited, a circle of cropped grass on the ground beside him. I brushed Silvereye, and I crooned to him and fed him a wheat cake before staking him in a grassier spot and heading back for Kesh. By the time I returned, Kieran lay sprawled out on a pallet, and Abelard sat at the table, smoking a pipe and staring into the fire.

"He was exhausted," Abelard said. "He found nothing, then?"

I shook my head and seated myself next to him. A strange idea came to me. Pulling the red flag from my pocket, I held it out for Abelard to examine. "I, too, am searching for my heritage. I know nothing of it. Have you ever seen this design before?"

Abelard spread out the flag and examined the swirling circles. My palms sweated, and my heart thudded heavily. I watched his eyes as he examined the flag, hoping against hope.

"I'm sorry, boy," he said. "It seems familiar, in some odd way, but I cannot say why. I have seen all manner of familial seals over the years . . . they run together in my mind. Perhaps I have never even seen it. I can tell you that if I have seen the design before, it is not in the records I have recovered so far."

My stomach plunged with disappointment. I shrugged, masking it. "It's all right, Speaker. Perhaps one day, I will find out. Perhaps not."

Abelard smiled warmly at me, but he did not comment. I had the unsettling notion that he could read my true emotion.

Just then, my stomach growled. Loudly. Abelard gave a merry laugh. "Your stomach voices what your mouth will not. Come, help me finish off the last of the soup."

I obliged him. It would have been rude to argue.

&

Kieran spent the entire next day in the ruined library, hunched over records, reading to himself. I wandered around outside for part of the day. Eventually, I approached a group of children and, striking up a conversation, questioned them about the Bel-Midron. The stories they told me of the monstrous Bel-Midron, who regularly stole their food, molested their women, and murdered any who defied them, upset me enough that I rushed back to Kieran's side. I remained there the rest of the day, practicing my sword moves and daydreaming about Shannon. When Abelard came for us, Kieran was so stiff that I had to help him upright. He walked in circles, cursing, until his muscles loosened.

"No luck again today, young sir?" Abelard questioned.

"Not a whit."

Abelard smoothed his beard over his chin. "Don't lose hope. What you're looking for is likely here, somewhere. Now, if you were looking for proof of royalty, that would be a different matter."

I looked at Kieran. His usual calm demeanor faded. I swallowed. Dear Shaddai. I wanted to trust Abelard . . . the man was a Speaker, after all.

I cleared my throat and spoke to Abelard's back as he led us from the library. "And if we were?"

Abelard gave a snort of laughter. "Well then you'd be in a bad spot! When it became clear that the Bel-Midron would take the city, Speaker Sheff and three of the acolytes packed up the royal records and escaped with them in the dead of night. They headed toward Citadel, but thieves stole their mounts and the speakers chased them halfway to Icefall before they were retrieved. By that time, they had word that Citadel was under siege, what with the War of Succession and all. Sheff traveled to Marden instead. That is where they remain today, still guarded by that old hound himself."

I felt like vomiting. Kieran, on the other hand, admirably restrained his disappointment.

"Really?" he said with forced civility. "I've never heard that the records resided there."

"I don't know why you would! Every year, Sheff sends a missive to Citadel, asking if the records can be kept there instead, but not once has his request been answered! It's fashionable for the nobility to keep their own libraries now, and the speakers there are too busy perfecting their red wine recipes to worry about learning. The rest of the country, now, they have a use for heritage records, which is why I stay on here. You'll see, though. One day, the nobles will have a need for those records and then no one will know where they are. Fools!"

"How do you know all this?" Kieran asked. He sounded more than a little accusatory. "Surely, you don't hear the latest news here in Kesh."

"Now that's where you're wrong, young sir. Sheff is my brother. Once a year, I travel to Verzon City to retrieve the letters he sends me every week."

Kieran halted in his tracks, and I ran into him. Abelard continued hurrying along, chattering. "Do you know what this means?" Kieran hissed in my ear.

It meant bad food and scrounging for firewood and huddling, wet and cold, on the bony back of a horse for months on end. It meant bright stars and cold wind and danger. It meant traveling north, to Marden, hundreds of miles distant.

Abelard scurried back to us. "Now don't get lost!" he scolded us.

We marched after him, numb and heartsick.

We were almost to Abelard's hut when the sound of a horn trumpeted through the air. Abelard stopped abruptly. "Shaddai help us!" He exhaled.

"What?" I asked, alarmed.

"Hurry, young sirs, inside my home!"

We rushed inside, and Abelard peered out of a dreary little hole that served as a window, muttering to himself.

"What is it?" I asked.

"Oh, young sirs. I'm afraid disaster has befallen us. The Bel-Midron have returned!"

Chapter Fourteen

The following afternoon, for the third time in a row, Kieran said, "Jutemeg." His voice was low and fierce.

"Is that an obscenity?" I asked with mild curiosity.

Kieran flattened his lips at me in annoyance. "Yes."

"Oh," I commented. Just that. I figured it would annoy Kieran further.

It did.

"What?" he asked.

"I don't think I've ever heard you curse before."

"Shut up, Lance."

I smiled and stretched out my feet atop a bench, appearing far more relaxed than I felt. We were in the library alone, listening to the faint cries of Bel-Midron warriors showing off their battle prowess in some nearby corner of the city. Kieran had thought it wise for us to pretend as though nothing was out of the ordinary when it came to our search for his heritage records. We somehow managed to do this even though neither of us had slept more than a few moments since last night. I don't know why teasing Kieran gave me perverse pleasure. I'd done my share of cursing as well since then.

When we'd come here in the morning, we agreed that leaving Kesh under cover of darkness seemed the only smart course to take. We debated leaving without Abelard's knowledge, but ultimately, we decided to lie to him instead.

When Abelard came for us at dusk, we met him smiling and fully packed. As we followed him back to his hut, Kieran told him the good news.

"Praise Shaddai that you have found what you sought!" Abelard cried.

"We will need your prayers to protect us as we leave tonight," Kieran said.

"Tonight?" Abelard exclaimed. "I fear, young sirs, that the Bel-Midron are especially dangerous tonight."

As we came upon Abelard's hut, a wild howl, followed by raucous laughter, pierced the air some distance away.

"They have been drinking all day—no, that's not true. Most of them were drunk when they returned, and none have sobered since then."

"Well, then, it may be easier to slip by them," Kieran said hopefully.

Abelard glanced at him askance. "You have not encountered a Bel-Midron in battle. I half think they are better skilled drunk than sober!"

We fell silent for a space, then, "I have an idea," Abelard burst out, leaping up to dig through a chest near the fireplace. He pulled out two moth-bitten brown habits. "You will wear these and go one at a time. If anyone sees, they'll think it's me! Unless, of course, they get a look at your faces. For Shaddai's sake, keep the hoods up and go one-by-one!"

I smoothed the rough fabric between my fingers. He was too poor to give us his clothing. He saw my expression and chided me, "It's no matter. Your lives are worth all that I own."

I nodded in gratitude and pulled the voluminous robes atop my clothing. The loose hood fit easily over my head, but the floppy sides obstructed my vision.

"Excellent!" Abelard exclaimed. "Come, let us find a place to conceal ourselves until the darkness becomes thicker."

Sunset allowed us just enough time to scramble over rocks and through deserted warrens, past whining hounds and the huts of crying children before we came to a mound of firewood that stood at the entrance to the marketplace. A desolate field lay directly in front of the dry creek bed that led to Silvereye and the plains beyond. At least a hundred Bel-Midron cavorted drunkenly around a huge bonfire, laughing and cursing, their silver medals and buckles clinking discordantly.

As the sky became slate gray, Abelard turned to Kieran. "Go, now, and go boldly. Lance will follow when it is safe."

The thought of him going alone made my stomach twist sickeningly. Kieran nodded and gripped Abelard's shoulder in goodbye. Then he gripped my shoulder with a warm, steady hand. I could not look into his eyes, but I could tell by his voice that they would be steady as well.

"Don't worry, Lance. The One will protect us if it is his will that we live."

I envied him his calm acceptance. I nodded and put my own hand on top of his for a moment. Then he was gone, moving in a quick, shambling imitation of Abelard's gait.

"Yes, my boy," Abelard whispered as he watched Kieran. "Yes, that is right. Move quickly, and do not keep too far to the shadows. They will become suspicious if they see that."

Kieran faded from my view, attracting no more than half-hearted shrieks and fist-shaking from several of the more intoxicated Bel-Midron. I waited in suspense for several more moments before relaxing in relief. Abelard, ever watchful, scanned the Bel-Midron, his lips moving in observation, "Yes, Mordell, continue to sample of the vine . . . yes, Ilkan, nurse your anger against Emek . . . look to him and not to us!"

I waited, silent and impatient, counting my breaths until I ran out of numbers and then counting them again. The night deepened, and someone brought out a musical instrument full of jangling bells, which brought a cheer of appreciation and rowdy singing.

"Now!" Abelard hissed. "While they are distracted with the music. Go quickly . . . they will think I am wandering again, as I often do at night!"

I rose, feeling numb all over. Abelard grasped my hand. "Shaddai bless and keep you, my young sir. May your journey be quick. And may you find what you seek, in all ways." He smiled, and I knew suddenly that he spoke of my family name, so long lost to me.

"Thank you," I whispered and left before my nerve fled.

My steps seemed as slow and ponderous as a turtle's. I concentrated on them, and not on my danger. The urge to run nearly overwhelmed me. I risked a look at the raiders, a hundred paces off, who were consumed with themselves and their drink.

I concentrated on moving.

"You! Stop!" A voice, harsh and loud. Female.

My heart stopped. My legs froze as though by her command. A curvy woman weaved toward me, earrings tinkling. In a moment, she literally stumbled into my arms. The heavy perfume of wine drenched her.

"Holy man," she slurred, eyes sleepy. "Off to pray? Give thanks for this." Her quick little hand smoothed my crotch. She laughed at my sharp intake of breath and reeled back toward the fire.

Eyes swiveled toward me, one man, in particular. Tall and hard, eyes tinted orange by the firelight, full beard threaded with medals that glinted like starlight. He had the bearing and aspect of a leader. I searched my memory for the name Abelard had given me for the head of this band. Searle. I held his gaze for a frozen instant before averting my eyes and shambling away. The drunken singers got louder, then dissolved into a chorus of laughter. Perhaps their mirth would draw Searle's attention from me.

"You! Holy man!" he shouted in a deep voice and rushed toward me through the grass and weeds.

Or perhaps not.

I halted, fear gushing up my throat like vomit. My sword hung over my shoulder, the hilt peeping through the neck hole of my garment. Though my first inclination was to run like a jack rabbit, the cursed long robes would trip me after about three steps. I snatched my sword from between my shoulder blades and swung at the approaching figure, crying, "Wrong, barbarian! I left his corpse back yonder, among the ruins."

I hoped that Abelard could hear my words. Perhaps this ruse would protect him, or give him time to escape, if nothing else. Searle leaped back in surprise, medals jangling. I smelled him from here— stale sweat, horse manure, and strong wine.

With one smooth movement, he pulled a long, thin dagger from his belt and spread his legs in a fighting stance. He smiled.

"He warned us that you would come and that you would bring the other one. The young one, like you, but dark-haired."

"You speak in riddles, tribesman."

"It matters not if you understand who brings you to your death as long as you cooperate with me and die."

Such a glib tongue in his foul mouth! I longed to cut it out. I slashed at him, making him dance backward on light feet. He laughed and feinted forward, quick as an adder. I could not spare even a glimpse for his drunken comrades.

Surely, Searle would summon help at any moment. But he did not. He stepped toward me and jabbed, coming dangerously close to puncturing my sword arm. I wielded my sword and drove him backward and sideways, to where the shadows deepened.

He avoided my blade and darted at me again, quick and lethal. This time, he pricked my forearm. My blade collided with his as he drew it back and produced a whistling shriek. Questioning sounds from the other drunkards indicated that they had noticed us.

"Back!" Searle shouted. "This one is mine alone!" And his fellows obeyed him, watching now from a distance.

We danced back and forth. All the while, I urged him backward and over, away from the firelight, which illuminated our blades with random glints. Each step improved my chances of survival, putting that much more distance between the others and us. Searle's annoying grin continued, not even wavering when I drove him back three steps at once—perhaps because in the next instant, he drove me back a like amount. I sweated and panted and worried that the others were not coming to Searle's aid not because of his command, but because he was playing with me.

Edging aside, I stumbled on a rock. With a cry, I went down on one knee. Searle's cursed grin widened. He had me now. We both knew it.

A loud crack sounded.

Doom?

Searle's eyes crossed, and he collapsed into a heap at my feet, revealing Abelard's wild-eyed figure. He held a branch as big as my arm.

"Go, young sir. Find Kieran. Don't delay!"

I jumped up. "But he'll come after you!"

"Then I'll brain him again!" Abelard declared. "Don't worry about me. Shaddai protects his own. Now, go!" He shook the stick at me.

I grasped his shoulder and squeezed, words escaping me. In the next moment, I hurried toward Kieran and life beyond. When I looked back, I saw that Abelard had melted into shadows.

I walked for nearly a mile when a sharp hiss identified Kieran, sitting astride Silvereye behind a bush. Dazed and grateful to have made it this far, I grasped his hand, and he hauled me up behind him in the saddle. Kieran nudged Silvereye in the ribs and we rode away, slowly at first, hampered by the pitch-dark night, only dimly lit by the crescent moon. When we came to the old royal road that led north from Kesh, Kieran kicked Silvereye into a gallop and we sped across the plains, the night wind warm across our faces. Silvereye tired quickly, and by the time his gait had returned to a steady walk, my heart had almost ceased its rapid beating.

I told Kieran about my encounter with Searle, including his strange words at our meeting.

"You think Searle knew to expect us?" Kieran asked. "How?"

Now that was a good question. One name came to mind. Morrigu. But I did not say it, and neither did Kieran.

We traveled far into the night, lapsing into silence. I drew imaginary patterns from star to star, like I used to as a boy, before nodding off, exhausted from the fight and the previous night's unrest. Despite waking from time to time to keep myself from resting against Kieran's back, I dreamed.

A storm billowed up around me, full of wind, dust, and cold rain that pelted me like tiny pebbles. A storm cloud, all dark and ominous and full of potent forces, hung in front of me. I flew through it, buoyed on wind. Lightning made eerie shadows on the cloud walls, and thunder vibrated the nothingness beneath my feet. The storm moved, taking me with it, charging the very air I breathed with energy and Power and a restless, relentless intelligence that seemed oddly familiar. I lifted my hands. My fingertips tingled, sizzling and burning, aching for me to let loose with an explosion of light and heat and—

I jerked awake.

The night was calm, quiet, and still except for the rhythmic sound of Silvereye's hooves crunching gravel. I made a fist. My fingertips burned and tingled. Odd.

The short nap had refreshed me. Kieran rode with his head nodding and his shoulders slumped. He didn't complain, but I knew how exhausted he must be. I traded places with him and let him rest his cheek against my back as he slept. He wakened just as dawn broke across the plains, and together, we watched the long golden fingers of morning eliminate the dark crevices of night. We stopped for a short rest, then scanned the barren land behind us for signs of Bel-Midron.

"Despite my fight with Searle, we made it out of Kesh without a scratch," I said with sudden revelation. "Surely, that bodes well for the remainder of our trip." The strange dream and the breaking morning had combined to invigorate me.

"I doubt it," Kieran said. He stood up, shielding his eyes and pointing eastward. "Someone is coming."

I jumped up, hurrying to his side. He was staring down the long, gentle hill we had so recently climbed. A solitary black figure made its way toward us. The gait of the horse seemed familiar.

I looked at Kieran in astonishment. He looked at me. Of one mind, we both cried, "Paddy!"

"How delightful," I said snidely. "He's coming directly toward us."

Kieran asked, "Why is he riding like he's being chased by a pack of devils?"

"Because he probably is."

The figure came closer as we stood, unmoving. Apparently, he recognized us, because he began waving frantically. What did the little devil expect after what he did to us? A warm reception? Neither Kieran nor I waved back. Still, I was glad to see him alive and well.

Shortly, he pulled his mount up in front of us and jumped off. Goldie stood gasping, froth forming around her mouth. Paddy didn't look much better. Sweat matted his hair and he trembled as he tried to catch his breath. Dirt caked his clothing, which was ripped in places, as if he'd dashed through a thorn bush. A bloody scrape marred one cheek and a goose egg stood out on his forehead.

"I can explain everything!" he blurted out.

I balled my hands on my hips. "Yes, please do."

"I'm in trouble."

"I agree," I said, glaring.

"I—" He lunged forward and threw his skinny arms around my waist, bursting into very un-Paddy-like sobs.

I stiffened. Kieran looked as surprised as I felt. Awkwardly, I patted his back, softening. "Stop crying. We won't hurt you. Don't you know that?"

Paddy sobbed for several more moments before choking out a tearful explanation.

"I lied to you 'bout my parents selling me to Moleck's men. My father has been dead since I was a baby. Now my mother is dead, too!" With this, he began wailing anew. I held him close against me, my heart freezing in my chest, until he cried himself out.

When he looked up at me, tears had cleared tracks down his dusty face. His upper lip quivered. Kieran handed him a handkerchief. He wiped off his face and took a moment to compose himself before taking a breath. "I am from the village, Shriversville, not many days' ride from here. The Bel-Midron never bothered us until a few months ago, when they attacked for no reason. It was awful. There was screaming and smoke and the cracking of whips. One of the raiders came into our tent. I tried to protect Mother, but he struck me in the back with his knife. When I awoke next, I was in my grandfather's cave. A few of the survivors had taken me there. They said that Mother was dead and they would not let me see her body. I didn't want to believe them. They tried to take me with them to another village in the north, but as soon as I was well enough, I ran away. That's when I found you." He paused, sniffling.

"You wanted to go to Kesh, which was near enough to our old village, so that's why I went with you. When we got close, I took Goldie and made it back to my village. The Bel-Midron were gone, but another group of men were there, evil priests who worship Moleck."

"How do you know they worship Moleck?" Kieran interrupted. "Perhaps they were Bel-Midron."

"They weren't," Paddy insisted. "I've seen them before. Grandfather told me who they were. He always told me to stay away from them because they are bad men. Anyhow, that's not what is important. What's important is that even though it took me all day, I crept into my old home. It had been burned, and there were bones inside. Mother's bones. I had your crossbow, Lance, so I took it outside and shot it at the priests of Moleck."

Naturally. He couldn't just run away like any other person. "How many did you hit?"

Paddy shrugged. "Three or four. They were surprised."

Realization dawned on me. "And now they are chasing you."

Paddy nodded miserably. Kieran and I met eyes. Back the way Paddy had come, a handful of riders topped the faraway ridge and headed our direction.

Paddy followed our gaze, exclaiming, "But I thought I lost them!"

We didn't even have time to curse.

I grabbed Paddy, and we mounted Silvereye. Kieran took Goldie, and we shot off to the west, riding as fast as we dared push the horses. The plains, the cursed, beautiful plains that had so reminded me of Lor, offered little in the way of cover. The priests wore dark robes and grim expressions, and their long-legged horses came from the finest stock.

"What has happened to my father's kingdom, Lance?" Kieran asked as we rode. "Evil priests, marauding Bel-Midron—it has become a wild place."

We lost the priests several times over the course of the next two hours, but like bloodhounds sniffing our trail, they spotted us again and again. We did not speak, but concentrated on pushing forward, farther and harder, urging the horses to the ends of their abilities. It would have been easier to just stop and fight them, but not with Paddy and Kieran along. I would not let either of them be hurt.

We stopped when we could, hidden in tiny culverts or behind outcroppings of brush, and poured water down our thirsty horses' throats, daring to let them catch a few breaths of rest. The priests were not so mindful of their mounts. I counted six of them, hooded and faceless, fully grown, powerful men who rode as if they had been birthed on horses. Perhaps they had.

Other times, we had no choice but to ride in the open, vulnerable but determined. I concentrated only on the next steps, but before long, I noticed a copse of trees ahead, clear and low in the noonday sun. Bog-country lay beyond, thick-wooded and concealing. Kieran glanced back at me, tight-faced, sunken-eyed, and he communicated a voiceless message to me. We would make for the copse and lose the priests there.

But the priests continued their advance, foot by slow foot, until I could make out the bright red scrollwork embroidered on their cloaks. I leaned low on Silvereye, Paddy's thin body before me, and breathed my will into Silvereye's ear.

Run! Don't stop. Run faster and farther.

He tried. I felt it in the focus of his steps, heard it in his tearing breath. His will remained strong, but his muscles could only push so far. He stumbled and snorted and righted himself again. This time, his gallop was slower. Shaddai! It became clear in the moments that followed that we would not make it to the copse in time.

Hooves closed on us. My stomach sank, then hardened. So be it. I would fight, to the death, if that's what it took. I leaned close to Paddy's ear and directed him, in a steady, calm voice, "When I tell you to, run as fast as you can into those trees. Do not stop, no matter what happens." He nodded, whimpering.

I held him close against my chest and pulled on Silvereye's reins, wheeling to face my nearest opponent, a wild-eyed priest whose robes snapped in the wind. His sword flashed, long and evil. Mine met his in an explosion of steel. I did not feel the force, nor my countering moves, which seemed so slow and precise. I heard only my breath, echoing like a harsh storm. The priest gave a sharp cry, unintelligible. Movement approached on my free side. Then, the whistling of a sword slicing through air, the flat of a blade. It cracked Silvereye's skull.

Silvereye screamed and twisted, and we went down. As we fell, I threw Paddy clear. Silvereye slid on the grass before landing heavily on my leg. Pain exploded, white hot. I cried out and tried to jerk my leg free, but it would not budge. Silvereye lay motionless. Paddy had landed on his feet nearby, agile as a cat.

"Lance—"

"Go!" I bellowed.

He obeyed with a last frightened look, running for the copse as fast as his skinny legs would carry him. My sword had bounced free of my hand in the fall, but by some stroke of luck, it had landed within reach. I snatched it up just as my opponent threw a leg over his saddle horn and leaped at me, his weapon poised to sink deep into my chest. Moving my arm upward in an arc, I knocked aside his blade. The priest's face collided with my shoulder and cheekbone. He rolled away, righting himself.

I glimpsed Kieran, frantically beating off a swarm of priests nearby. Shaddai! There were too many of them. I scrabbled at the ground with my free hand, trying to extricate my trapped leg from under the horse. Pain seared through me, and I made no progress. Silvereye was *heavy*. Motion behind me. The priest came at me from behind so that I had to twist my neck to see him. He gave a harsh laugh as I swung my sword frantically, with limited range. Our swords met again in a thunderous confrontation, and mine broke in half. Part of it flew wide, tumbling through the air with odd slowness. The priest sneered at me, his eyes cruel and black.

With both hands, the priest brought his blade down. I tried to twist aside—too late. The blade plunged into my torso. Muscles tore. Pain. Blood colored my side. Kieran screamed my name. The sound reverberated through my ears and into my mind.

The battle had been short. Too short. Nausea spun me in a circle, stealing my senses. Down I fell, wheeling, into a black, soundless pit.

Chapter Fifteen

Sobbing and shaking wrenched me out of blissful unconsciousness.

"Lance!" the wail sounded, traveling all the way down the black pit I had been sleeping in. "Lance! Wake up. Don't be dead, please!"

Someone was shaking my shoulders.

I opened my eyes. Bright light. Blue Sky. Paddy, kneeling in front of me, tears pouring down his cheeks. He shook me as hard as his skinny little arms could manage.

"I'm not dead!" I snapped, and the shaking finally stopped.

I sat up as well as I could with Silvereye draped over my leg. The plains were empty save for scuffed up grass and a sword, lying bloody and chipped, near my hand.

Paddy pointed at the sword. He shrieked, "He left it in you! I just pulled it out."

My jerkin was torn at my side. A gash ran along my ribs, shallow but bloody. I must have twisted away just enough to save my innards. I squeezed Paddy's shoulder. "It's not bad at all. A bit of moss on the wound and I'll be good as ever."

What about poor Silvereye, then? I put my hand on his spine. As if in answer to my question, he snorted, shook his head, and scrambled clumsily to his feet.

I laughed out loud. "He's not dead either! We fooled them, Paddy!"

Paddy didn't look entirely convinced. I ran my hands down my leg . . . no broken bones. When I tried to move, the blood began coursing through my veins again. Shaddai in heaven, it hurt! It took a few moments of grunting and groaning and blinding pain, but Paddy grabbed my arm and tugged until I stood upright, slightly lopsided. I ran my hands over Silvereye, looking for injuries, but other than a huge lump by his ear, he seemed unscathed.

"Kieran?" I asked.

"He's gone."

"Where? Is he hurt?" I heard no voice in my mind, felt no speechless presence at my side. The loneliness of that loss surprised me.

"I don't know! I ran into the bushes like you told me to, so I couldn't see much. They came looking for me after they thought they'd killed you, but I hid in a good place. I didn't come out until it was safe, and by then, they were gone."

I bit my lip, worried. "So they've taken him somewhere. How long have I been out?"

"Not long. A half hour—maybe an hour. I'm not sure. They went east. That's all I know."

"Good. That helps. Come on, we must go after them."

I turned to help him climb atop Silvereye when my brain exploded in waves of grief and anger, pain and indignation. I stumbled, crashing to my knees and clutching my head. Gale force winds, fist-sized hail, fire from heaven . . . nothing compared with the sound–color–light of the emotions slamming against my skull from the inside out. Then, recognition.

Kieran! You're blasting my mind out!

The sea of emotion stopped churning.

Lance? I sensed his breath, held back, and his mind, reeling with shock and disbelief.

Yes, it's me. Who else can you communicate with like this?

Lance! His cry accompanied such an overwhelming burst of relief and happiness that it, too, hurt my head. Yet, I couldn't keep myself from smiling and even laughing out loud.

You're alive! Kieran sent. *I thought they'd killed you—*

Never mind about me. Where are you? Are you injured?

I'm fine, for now. I'm east of you. I don't know how far. They haven't told me who they are working for, but I know it's him.

Who?

Morrigu. I think he leads the priests of Moleck who took me. They've been looking for me for a long time. They found me by reading Paddy's thoughts, then they followed him because of revenge, yes, but also to get to me.

The length and breadth of Morrigu's power sent spears of icy terror through me.

By the One, Lance, these priests of his frighten me as well, Kieran sent, startling me by perceiving my fear. *They've come from nowhere, and they seem so well-organized and determined. And—wait! They're talking and pointing.* He paused, his attention directed elsewhere. I waited, suspended by the silent hold of his consciousness. When I felt his attention return to me, it was like pure, warm sunlight after a chill rainstorm. *We're coming up on something. It looks like a chasm gouged in the Land. It's hard to see. I'm lying head down over the saddle and my arms are tied in front of me.* His violent surprise pitched my stomach forward. *No! It's not possible. There are so many of them.*

A great dizziness came over me, and I felt my contact with Kieran slipping away. Damn it. Not now!

Kieran! I forced my will and concentration into a single, panicked cry.

But the Power didn't respond, fickle and cruel. Whether it was his fault or mine, or no one's at all, I couldn't say.

Then, a final, weak connection, distant and faint.

I'm coming for you! I managed to send. The connection slipped away entirely.

I opened my eyes back to reality, feeling panicked and angry and sick to my stomach.

Paddy frowned at me. "Don't you think it's about time you tell me what's going on?"

"Not now. We've got to go. Grab Silvereye."

Paddy led Silvereye to me. I shoved aside my worry and took a moment to pat him on the neck. "Sorry, boy. I wish I could give you more rest."

He turned his great head to nuzzle my neck. He, too, would gladly give up his life for Kieran. Jealousy surged up inside me, unbidden and unwanted. I calmed the emotion with truth. Kieran deserved such sacrifice, even if I didn't.

We took off at a lumbering trot toward the east. Anger simmered in my chest, deep, strong, and alive. I kept my eyes fixed on the Land ahead of us, following an invisible trail to Kieran. Silvereye picked up speed, as though drawing fuel from my impatience.

My head ached, and my battered, exhausted body tensed like iron. Purpose and grim-lipped determination filled me. But beneath these feelings lay a timeless sort of knowing that guided me onward, straightaway, to Kieran's location and the unfolding of my destiny.

We came to the chasm nearly an hour later. It opened across the smooth rolling earth like a jagged scar, deep and uneven, with rocky walls and a path zigzagging down to the bottom, where great plumes of white steam issued from a fissure that must have plumbed the depths of eternity itself. A table-like structure stood near it. One of the famed 'altars of the east', I presumed. Black-cloaked priests milled about a prone figure wearing fawn-colored breeches. Kieran. From this distance, I could not tell whether he still lived and breathed.

Pausing Silvereye at the lip of the chasm, I reached and lifted Paddy, stringy and light, to the ground. I couldn't let him stay with me. It was just too dangerous. He didn't resist me. He just looked up with a calm expression.

"You can't keep me here. I'll follow you even if we both go to our deaths. I won't be alone again." His voice caught on the word, *alone.*

I regarded him, so small and sincere. My rational mind told me to tie him to a tree if that's what it took to keep him safe. Knowing the little urchin, he'd

200

probably chew through the ropes before I made it halfway down the hill.

I lifted him back into the saddle behind me. "You've got crossbow detail. Make sure you get as many of those vipers as possible."

Looking at the chasm, I took a deep breath. I could see only one way to do this, and that was without delay.

I sent Silvereye down the zigzagging path at a healthy canter. We made it at least halfway there before the first of the priests saw us and cried out. A lot of shouting and clattering ensued, and within a few blinks of an eye, a mob of the priests came flying at us. A quick count totaled twenty-three priests and one angry king-to-be, bound hand and foot and propped against the altar.

"Get out of here, Lance!" he shouted, in both my ears and my mind.

Although I was aware of his anger and exasperation with my unimaginative tactics, the mind-speak did not overwhelm me like before. It stayed in its own place in my head, barricaded behind something huge and growing like a summer thunderhead.

Two of the priests aimed nocked arrows at us.

"Down!" I shouted to Paddy.

One of the arrows whizzed across my back so closely that I felt the puff of air it created.

I kicked Silvereye into a gallop. We collided directly with a knot of priests running for their weapons. At least two of the priests fell beneath Silvereye's hooves. The sound of bones snapping and crunching was distinct.

Paddy got off two crossbow bolts. One struck a priest in the meat of his thigh before the priests surrounded us and pulled at him with their hands. He clung to my waist like a tumor. I grabbed one of the priests by his oily thatch of hair and yanked him upward. When he was high enough, I plucked the sword out of his fist, then shoved him back with a tremendous kick. That caused the group to retreat for a breath, then they surged at us again like pooling water.

I slashed and hacked like a maniac, cracking a skull here and busting an arm there, yelling and cursing. Our abrupt appearance had so surprised the priests that only about half of them had managed to grab their weapons. The other half used their bare hands to strike at us or try to pull us from Silvereye. With Paddy restricting my movement, I couldn't knock heads as effectively as I wanted. Still, I managed to skewer a bald-headed enemy before succumbing to the grasping hands and tumbling off Silvereye. Paddy released me. I fell one way, and he fell the other. Free of Paddy's weight, I leaped up and engaged the priests on foot. They fanned back like frightened deer. Several of the bolder, armed priests detached from the others, and I took on three fighters at once.

A vicious blow slammed into my wrist, causing my fingers to spasm unwillingly. My sword went flying, and the priests closed around me.

A short laugh from Kieran's direction halted them in their tracks.

"A good effort, Lance of Lor. But pitifully lacking."

Shaddai, that voice sounded familiar.

I looked over to see Searle, the Bel-Midron leader, crouching next to Kieran with his knife pressed to my friend's neck. Kieran's eyes met mine. I swallowed, my mouth dry.

Searle tugged Kieran to his feet. Moisture from the nearby steam column matted Kieran's hair and soaked the front of his tunic.

"You never really had a chance," Searle continued and gestured toward the canyon walls, so close and tall.

Dozens of Bel-Midron warriors emerged from well-camouflaged caves, crannies and trails scattered up and down the canyon walls.

"How pathetic," I said, angry and desperate. "The once-fearsome Bel-Midron now bow before the foul priests of Moleck."

"We bow before no one, boy. We are allies who seek the Power of the Void and Chaos, those dark opposites of the Land and the Law."

"Is that how you know my name? Did you hear it from the lips of the Evil One himself?" I asked.

"Oh, no. He has no lips. Yet. I heard it from a far more earthly source. The same one who told me to sacrifice the fledgling king here."

"Let me guess. Morrigu."

"As such."

Everything happened at once, then. Searle's arm flexed in preparation for slicing Kieran's throat. With a cry, Kieran shoved Searle away, ducking out from under his arms. Several priests rushed to pin him down. Meanwhile, I sprang toward Searle.

Searle tossed aside his knife and tugged a sword from the sheath at his waist. Our blades met with a furious clang. Our chests collided, faces within inches of one another. I smelled his rank body odor and sour breath and felt the cool metal from the medals in his beard.

I shoved him, snarling, but succeeded in moving him only a few feet. Human strength. Human weakness!

I slashed at Searle with an angry cry, missed, and struck the red-brown soil. Damn it. Drawing back in a full arc, I struck harder and met unyielding steel.

We parried back and forth, grunting and sweating at a furious pace. I went forward a step, backward two, my body a taut wire and his a granite column. His strength and will, undimmed now by alcohol, surprised me.

Strike, smash, jab, feint.

He slammed me hard on the upper arm.

Rage churned inside, hot and wild. I jabbed him in the shoulder with a bruising, off-center hit.

He smiled, just like he had last night before we fought. Then he elbowed me away and kicked at my knee with his hard boot.

I whirled around, evading his strike, and our blades clashed again. Strike, retreat, match, slash. My eyes stayed on him, the world around a chaotic blur.

Inside, something rose. Something inevitable and awesome, with a life of its own.

Searle's eyes flicked in Kieran's direction.

"Slit his throat, boys!" he cried.

My rage became primal. Unstoppable. It consumed my muscles, burned my blood, and burst out of my chest. Real, alive, and vengeful.

Power.

The immensity of it! Surging, building, erupting. It came from me, but *not* from me. It was too great—too immense—to come from my human form.

It had a life of its own, and desires. It wanted. What? *Release.*

Smoke. Fire.

Release me.

I did.

The Power took me.

I pointed my sword in Searle's direction. A great, crashing noise sounded, as if the Land itself shrieked in rage.

Lightning shot from my chest to my outstretched arm. It leapt off the end of my sword, zigzagging through the air to impact squarely on Searle's chest. Shock imprinted on his face as he flew through the air. Arms windmilling, he landed heavily twenty feet away. A black hole smoked in the middle of his chest. He lay still. Dead.

Madness seized me. Lightning shot out in all directions.

Sound all around, crashing and screaming. The altar split down the center and caught fire. Anger and vengeance rolled through me in god-like waves.

No, not waves. *Winds.*

Three tornadoes shot from my outstretched fingers. The tiny mortals cried out in terror, their faces twisted. They turned and ran, but they could not escape me. Black-cloaked bodies flew aside. Ten, twenty. And others, ragged warriors with long hair. I spun them backward, smashed them into cliff walls, and sent them tumbling from their primitive caves to the hard earth below. Men pushed each other aside to flee my wrath. Disgusting creatures, desperate and grasping. Some had already made it up the dirt pathway to the top of the chasm.

I summoned wind to raise me up, light and steady, through air that sizzled with Power, until I came to rest at the top of the chasm. I met the first man exiting the trail. He greeted me with a look of horror. A gesture from my hand sent the winds against him and the others behind him. Bodies sailed to the earth below, some never to rise again, others scrambling off, injured and moaning.

I was infinite in strength and purpose. What did I care for these weak creatures who inhabited my skin for such a short time? They were a breath, here and then gone. And they dared to defy me. I would crush the life from all of them.

Yet something held me back.

If I killed them all, I would also kill the nameless young man, calm and blessed in the midst of the tempest. Who was he? I should know him . . .

Reasoning burst upon me. Kieran! I might hurt him or the boy.

As suddenly as it had come, the lightning evaporated and the wind fled from my fingertips. Abruptly, I became only human again, a small, insignificant human. My legs buckled, and I flopped on the ground like a wet rag, face first in the dust. Several priests and at least one Bel-Midron ran past my prone form.

Familiar voices sounded from somewhere down below.

My head spun, and the world whirled around me in nauseating circles. I breathed in short bursts, sending up little plumes of dust. Paddy ran up from somewhere and tugged at me until he turned me over. When he saw that I wasn't dead, he muttered something about getting the horses. He ran off again. Kieran appeared, dust-covered and wind-blown. He pressed a wine skin to my lips.

I sat up, coughing and holding my head in my hands. The world didn't stop spinning for a long moment. When it did, I saw Kieran staring at me with a silent, pale face.

I peered over the edge of the chasm and around me. Bodies lay about. Lightning had scorched the ground, and wind had ripped up bushes and flattened grass. Did this come from inside me?

I couldn't bear the immensity of the answer.

We stared at each other in mute silence. I remembered my dream of wind and lightning several hours ago.

Kieran said, "The evil that the monks warned me of all those months ago, Lance. It was the return of the priests of Moleck and their alliance with the raiders. You destroyed that alliance here today."

"Don't be so sure of that," said a sibilant voice from no more than ten feet away.

Morrigu! Complete with his dark purple cape. I fell back, shocked. His figure was ghost-like, translucent in spots. Hatred radiated from his face.

"The alliance remains," Morrigu sneered. "And every day, our forces grow stronger. What you have done here is a temporary inconvenience."

Morrigu blinked out of existence. A warm puff of air that smelled like sulfur ruffled our hair.

"Tell me this has all been a bad dream."

"I wish it were," Kieran replied.

Paddy came up the trail leading Silvereye, Goldie, and one of the priests' horses, a scruffy black gelding. I got to my feet and tottered over to Silvereye, clinging to his saddle until my strength returned.

Finally, Paddy said, "That was a strange storm. Can we go now?"

I gaped at him. Kieran did the same. We met eyes then, and simultaneously burst out laughing. Paddy looked from one of us to the other, his face twisted in irritation.

"What's so funny? Are we leaving or not?" He pointed down into the chasm, where the few remaining Bel-Midron and priests of Moleck had huddled together. "They are going to come out sooner or later."

"Without their leaders, they won't be much trouble."

"You'll stay with us, then?" Kieran looked at Paddy.

"It's not like I have anywhere else to go," Paddy snapped.

"Then, to Marden it is, to find answers," Kieran said, then he looked at me and smiled. "Let us ride, my Champion."

I mounted Silvereye. What wonders had happened here today, and in the past months.

How had a nameless bastard ended up a king's man on a journey across mountains and dark rivers into the unknown?

With a wild shout, I kicked Silvereye into a gallop, and we dashed across the plains, toward the mountains of tomorrow.

Book Two of The King's Champion Series

Trials by Sword

Coming Spring 2018

Join author Xina Marie Uhl's monthly mailing list at http://eepurl.com/DoEz5 for notification about upcoming releases, special offers, and free fiction.

About The Author

Xina Marie Uhl spends her days laboring in obscurity as a freelance writer for educational projects and dreaming of ways to scrounge up enough cash to: 1. travel the world, and 2. add to her increasing menagerie of dogs, cats, and other creatures. The rest of the time she writes fantasy, romance, historical fiction, and humor.

You can find her on Facebook, Twitter, and WordPress, where she writes about historical research, writing, and whatever strikes her fancy.

Join the author's monthly newsletter at http://eepurl.com/DoEz5 for character artwork, exclusive fiction, and up-to-date news on the release of Book Two in the King's Champion series, *Trials by Sword*.

A Word to the Reader

If you've made it this far, and you enjoyed the book, why not review it? Short or long, your review helps to spread the word about the series.

www.ingramcontent.com/pod-product-compliance
Lightning Source LLC
Chambersburg PA
CBHW072227190626
46809CB00017B/1017